JERRY TODD'S
POODLE PARLOR

'QUICK!" CRIED PEG. "DIVE INTO THE HAY, FELLOWS."

Jerry Todd's Poodle Parlor   *Frontispiece (Page 190)*

JERRY TODD'S POODLE PARLOR

By
LEO EDWARDS

AUTHOR OF
THE JERRY TODD BOOKS
THE POPPY OTT BOOKS

ILLUSTRATED BY
MYRTLE SHELDON

GROSSET & DUNLAP
PUBLISHERS   NEW YORK

TO
MY PAL
NESTOR SMITHBACK

CONTENTS

LEO EDWARDS' BOOKS

Here is a list of Leo Edwards'
published books:

THE JERRY TODD SERIES

JERRY TODD AND THE WHISPERING MUMMY
JERRY TODD AND THE ROSE-COLORED CAT
JERRY TODD AND THE OAK ISLAND TREASURE
JERRY TODD AND THE WALTZING HEN
JERRY TODD AND THE TALKING FROG
JERRY TODD AND THE PURRING EGG
JERRY TODD IN THE WHISPERING CAVE
JERRY TODD, PIRATE
JERRY TODD AND THE BOB-TAILED ELEPHANT
JERRY TODD, EDITOR-IN-GRIEF
JERRY TODD, CAVEMAN
JERRY TODD AND THE FLYING FLAPDOODLE
JERRY TODD AND THE BUFFALO BILL BATHTUB
JERRY TODD'S UP-THE-LADDER CLUB
JERRY TODD'S POODLE PARLOR

THE POPPY OTT SERIES

POPPY OTT AND THE STUTTERING PARROT
POPPY OTT'S SEVEN-LEAGUE STILTS
POPPY OTT AND THE GALLOPING SNAIL
POPPY OTT'S PEDIGREED PICKLES
POPPY OTT AND THE FRECKLED GOLDFISH
POPPY OTT AND THE TITTERING TOTEM
POPPY OTT AND THE PRANCING PANCAKE
POPPY OTT HITS THE TRAIL
POPPY OTT & CO., INFERIOR DECORATORS

THE NEW POPPY OTT DETECTIVE STORIES

THE MONKEY'S PAW

JERRY TODD'S POODLE PARLOR

CHAPTER I

BUSINESS PLANS

THIS new story of mine starts with the start of our summer vacation in the little town of Tutter, Illinois, where I was born and raised.

The last week of school had been packed with final examinations, hurried programs and class picnics, as is usually the case with small-town public schools, but now everything about the old red brick schoolhouse had been closed up tight for the summer.

Oh, boy! I'll never forget how happy we were as we started out from Tutter that first morning of our vacation in Dad's old brickyard dump-cart. We were on our way to the old Windmere hotel, south of town, to get some lumber that we needed to carry out a scheme of ours.

There were three of us in the scheme—Red Meyers, Horse Foot Rail and myself—all lined up now on the narrow seat of the two-wheeled dump-cart with Red in the middle driving.

"Say, Jerry Todd," he presently spoke to me, as old Prince jogged along the sun-baked country road, "how much lumber do you think we'll get for our two dollars? Do you think we'll get enough to build the little candy store we've planned?"

"It's all old lumber," I told him, "so we certainly ought to get several times as much for our money as we would new lumber. But why puzzle about that till we get there? Boy, get a load of that blue sky up there! Look at those bluffs down there by the river, too! Aren't they pretty? We couldn't possibly have had a finer start for our summer vacation."

"Yes," Red spoke as happily, "it looks like this is going to be a grand summer for us, with our store and everything. But tell me, Jerry," he lowered his voice, "are you really going to give Horse Foot a third of the profits?"

"Of course," I declared. "He coaxed his ma into letting us build the store in his front yard, after your own ma and mine both turned us down. So he's certainly entitled to an equal share."

During the time that we had been talking, the Tutter church steeples had disappeared into the treetops behind us. We were almost to the Illinois River now, which we had to cross. Beyond the river our course lay by a big sanitarium on the shore of a beautiful little lake with wonderful scenery all around it. City people came by the hundreds to spend the summer months there, and in the big Woodlawn Bay hotel near there.

The Woodlawn Bay hotel and the old Windmere house stood side by side on the south river bank, each with about fifty acres of rolling wooded land around it. It was the new hotel, with its modern conveniences, that had put the old hotel out of business. Now, after years of idleness, the old hotel was being torn down and its lumber and fixtures sold for whatever they would bring.

Scoop Ellery, another chum of mine, had told me that the old Windmere house was being torn down. If I wanted to buy some old lumber for a little store building, he said, there was the place to get it cheap. I asked him then if he didn't want to go in with us, but he had gotten himself a vacation job with some woman with a bunch of summer cabins. He was going to be bellboy or something—he wasn't quite sure what yet, but he had been promised five dollars a week and his board. Later I heard that big Peg Shaw, the final member of my five-cornered gang, had gotten a summer job there, too, which made it look as though the old gang was going to be pretty much broken up for the summer. Big surprises were ahead of us though!

I'll come to Scoop pretty soon, telling you more about him then, and then later on in my story I'll better introduce Peg. But right now I want to tell you a little bit more about Red and Horse Foot.

Given the fancy name of Donald Henry at the time of his birth, Red gets his nickname from his fiery red hair. He has freckles, too, and a mouth that spreads all over his face, especially when he gives one of those impish grins of his. There was a time when I thought he was the meanest kid in our block, but today we get along swell. That's why you find him in all of my books. Whatever I'm in, he's in, too—one of the best buddies that any boy could ever have anywhere.

Of Horse Foot I can't say so much—at least I

can't be so enthusiastic about it.   Younger than me by at least two years, he got into my gang when he recently moved next door to me.   His real name is Samuel Horace Butterfield Rail, but we call him Horse Foot because when he's out with us he always plods along behind like an old heavy-footed plow horse.

I'll never forget the first day he came over to my house.   With that expressionless fat face of his, and his numerous fat bulges, all I could think of was something made out of putty.   I thought then, as I grinned at him amused, that he had just dropped in to say hello, in his stuttering way, and that would be the last of him.   I was soon to learn though that I couldn't turn around without having him at my heels. Oh, oh, how I suffered that first month!   I had to take it though, Mother having told me that I must never slight him or do anything that might cause him to carry home angry stories about me.   He looked so blamed stupid and had such a hard time with his speech, she was afraid his parents might be overly sensitive about him and liable to take offense if any trouble came up.

So wherever I went he went, too.   I thought at first that he was absolutely cuckoo but came to learn in time that a lot of his dumbness was just put on. In fact there were times, I found out, when he was downright brilliant.   He had grit, too.   He'd tackle anything.

Crossing the long river bridge, we turned, still laughing and talking, into the winding lake road, passing first the richly-appointed sanitarium on the lake shore, then the showy Woodlawn Bay hotel on the river bank, turning finally into the weedy Windmere hotel road.

Horse Foot had been sitting half-asleep all the way over, but awoke now, with a frightened squawk, when a low-hanging branch from one of the trees that had crowded in when the old road was abandoned almost slapped him off his seat.

"A-a-are we lost?" he asked, looking around surprised.

"That's just what I'm beginning to wonder myself," put in Red, as the road narrowed to a mere trail. "Are you sure this is the right road, Jerry?"

"Of course it's the right road," I kept on, old Prince picking his way first to the right and then to the left to avoid the crowding bushes. "The old hotel is directly east of the Woodlawn Bay hotel, isn't it?—and this is the first road since we passed the Woodlawn Bay road. The old hotel's just down around that bend, I think."

Here a familiar black head popped out of the left thicket. It was Scoop Ellery in a nifty blue bellboy uniform with a squirming fox terrier in his arms. There was a stare all around as our eyes met, Scoop as much surprised as the rest of us over the unexpected meeting.

"Oh, boy!" he leaned wearily against the side of the cart. "Am I ever hungry! Peg and I got here on our bikes at five-thirty and we've been on the jump every minute since."

"But I didn't understand that your cabins were down in this woods," I told him, surprised. "I thought you said they were on a farm."

"They are—I just came in here to run down this

crazy four-legged soupbone. Every time he gets loose he makes a beeline for this woods.   The cabins are over that way, on the old Beesaddle farm," Scoop pointed east.

"What farm did you say?" Red pricked up his ears at the odd name, grinning.

"The old Beesaddle farm," Scoop repeated. "Peg and I are working for a Mrs. Flora Beesaddle. There's a Mr. Beesaddle over there, too—Pappy Jim, she calls him—but he doesn't amount to much, the lazy old coot! She's the boss—*and how!* Boy, can she find jobs for a fellow! She's down there by the old hotel now picking out lumber for more cabins."

"Is that her dog?" I asked, as Scoop struggled with it to hold it.

"No, it belongs to one of the cabin renters.   I've had to run it down four times already this morning. Boy, wherever you go over there there's dogs, cats or something!   I never saw so many pets in all my life.   Peg and I thought at first this morning that we had gotten into some kind of a zoo."

"Well, you wouldn't have been very much out of place if you had," Red put in slyly.

"How do you like my uniform?" Scoop asked, stepping back to better show it off.

"Swell," I told him.   "You ought to wear it to town some day and give the girls a treat."

"Yes," Red slyly slipped in again, "with those brass buttons maybe you could even get a date. Girls usually fall hard for a uniform, regardless of what's in it."

"Listen, funny face!" Scoop soured up.   "You're

going to find that freckled nose of yours pushed
through the back of your head, if I hear another
wisecrack like that."

"Oh, never mind him," I told Scoop quickly.
"Tell us some more about your job, and how you
happen to have so many pets over there."

"S-s-sure thing," chimed in Horse Foot. "Tell
us some m-m-more about Mrs. Bumblebee."

"I didn't say Mrs. Bumblebee," laughed Scoop.
"I said Mrs. Beesaddle. Half the time though
Peg and I do call her Mrs. Bumblebee. She has
a scheme all her own, fellows. She rents specially
to rich people with pampered pets. Gee, they're a
funny bunch! I never thought that people could get
so daffy over pets."

"It sure sounds like an original scheme," I com-
mented.

"How much do you think the owner of this dog
pays for its board?" Scoop asked.

"A dollar a week?" I guessed.

"A *dollar* a week!" snorted Scoop. "She pays
five weeks a week, with another twenty-five on top
of it for her own board. Multiply that by eight—
for there are eight cabins over there—and you'll get
a rough idea of how much Mrs. Beesaddle is making. Her guests are all a strictly high-class bunch,
let me tell you. In one of the cabins there's an
actress with a cranky parrot, and this morning I
heard the others talking about getting up a play
around her. She's sixty if she's a day, but she trips
around in girlish clothes trying to make the others
think she's sweet sixteen. She wants them to put
on Romeo and Juliet, so she can get up in the bal-

cony with a lover.   The Cookbook Woman in number four also wants to be in the play.   Boy, it ought to be a 'yowling' success if she puts all her seventeen pet cats in it, too!"

"But why do you call her the Cookbook Woman?" I asked curiously.

"Because she's named all her cats out of a cookbook—Gingersnap, Soda Biscuit, and clear on down the line to Strawberry Shortcake."

"Howard!" a voice here called up ahead. "Where are you?"

"Oh-oh!" gurgled Scoop, ducking, as a tall mannish woman suddenly came into sight in the road. "That's Mrs. Bumblebee now.   Don't tell her I've been loafing here or I'll catch Hail Columbia."

The woman stopped us when we came up.

"Whose horse and cart is that?" she asked sharply.

"My father's," I told her, keeping the smile that was inside of me out of sight—for she did look like a fierce overgrown bumblebee.

"You're those Tutter boys, aren't you?" she asked further, scowling.

"Yes, we're from Tutter," I informed politely.

"Humph!   Well," she snapped into action, "you aren't going to get any lumber here—you little toughies!   So turn around and get out of here just as quickly as you can."

We thought she had stopped us to ask us about Scoop.   We never dreamed she was going to light into us that way.   For a minute or two all we could do was to sit there and stare at her.

But I got my voice back in a jiffy when she grimly

took old Prince by the bridle and started turning him around, the cart tipping perilously.

"Hey, don't do that!" I yelled, jumping up angrily. "We have a right to come in here if we want to. Let go of my horse."

But do you think I could stop her? Hardly! Turning Prince clear around, she marched him with long mannish strides back to the highway, heading him west toward Tutter.

"Now," she snapped at us, "git! And if I ever catch you in here again I'll shake you out of your pants. You can tell Mr. Norning, too, that I caught you in here and put you out. Did you hear me?" she took another heavy threatening step toward us. "I said to git."

CHAPTER II

AT THE OLD HOTEL

RATTLING quickly off in the cart, with Red and Horse Foot gaping back, we got safely out of the farm woman's sight and then stopped beside the road to talk matters over.

"What in Sam Hill do you make of that?" I asked the others, completely dumfounded myself.

"It's easy to see what her game is," growled Red. "She wants all the old lumber down there for herself to build more cabins with. And just because we're boys she thought she could scare us out."

"S-s-she did too," piped Horse Foot, with a vixenish look at Red. "Y-y-you sure were white, Red. Your freckles stood out like the polka dots in m-m-my Sunday necktie."

"Oh, yeah?" Red pushed out his chin, brave as a lion again. "If anybody happens to ask you, squash-face, she didn't scare me a bit. But you can't argue with an old cross-patch! Boy, I'd hate to work for her all summer, like Scoop and Peg! But give me those lines, Jerry. I'm going back and get that lumber, just as we planned. I'm not going to let her bluff me out."

I was just as determined as he was to get the lumber, but knew better than to go back then.

"A better plan," I suggested, "will be to wait here for ten or fifteen minutes and then sneak back afoot to see where she is. If she's over to her farm, then we'll race back for the cart and get in to the old hotel and out again with our lumber as fast as we can."

"But what if she went back to the old hotel?" Red asked.

"In that case we'll just have to wait till she's safely out of there. We can easily outwit her if we try. Toughies, huh?" I gave the insult more thought, my eyes narrowing. "Boy, I resent that! We've never done anything around here to get a reputation like that. So why should she call us toughies?"

"You've got too good an opinion of yourself," snorted Red, jumping out. "Maybe a lot of people have called us toughies, for all we know. It doesn't worry me. Come on," he swaggered off down the road, "I'm going to show her what a tough buzzard I really am."

"Listen here, Red," I went at him sharply, when I caught up with him, Horse Foot having been left behind to take care of the horse, "don't you sass that woman now, if we should happen to clash with her again. If she wants to be ill-mannered to us let her, but we'll show her that we aren't the toughies she said. Our folks wouldn't like it if we sassed her— we'd hear plenty about it if the story ever got back to town. So let's not do anything we'll be sorry for."

"But doesn't it make you boiling mad, Jerry?" he stamped along, himself burning indignantly to the tips of his freckled ears.

"Sure it does," I confessed. "She had no right to yank us out of there that way—it wasn't her prop-

erty. As you said, she took advantage of us because we're boys—wanting the lumber for herself.
But there's no use getting mouthy about it. The
thing to do is to keep cool and fool her if we can.
If we can do that and get the lumber we need in spite
of her, I'll be satisfied."

"Will the lumber be all piled up ready for us
when we get there?" Red asked eagerly.

"Oh, sure! There'll be a carpenter there, too,
to take the money—a Mr. Charley Kelly, Scoop
told me. But let's go quietly now," I lowered
my voice cautiously, "for we're almost to the old
road again, and she may be waiting for us there with
a stick."

"Do you see her?" Red breathed in my ear, as
we crept through the bushes.

"No," I breathed back. "She's either gone on
home or back down the old road to the hotel."

"She probably thought we were so scared that
we'd gallop old Prince all the way home," Red
chuckled.

"I guess we did look pretty scared when we drove
off," I laughed. "But shall we try the old hotel
first, to see if she's there, or go on over to her pet
farm?"

Red's eyes began to dance at mention of the farm
and the stories we had just heard about it.

"I'd like to see some of those cats and dogs," he
spoke eagerly.

"So would I," I confessed.

"Then let's go over there first," he suggested.

"O. K.," I agreed.

Directly across the highway from us was a small

neglected private cemetery. I noticed it but gave it very little thought just then, though later on it was to come prominently into my story. My eyes at the time were mostly turned down the old hotel road. There was no one in sight there, however, and crossing quickly we kept on through the bushes to the wood's edge, where the Windmere property ended and the Beesaddle farm land began. Leaving the highway there, to the left, for better cover, we worked guardedly around to another scattered grove between the farm buildings and the near-by river, coming finally to the barn. All around were hundreds of chickens and ducks that probably would go into the pot before the summer was over to feed the guests there. We saw several Jersey cows, too, contentedly chewing their cuds in the shade.

It couldn't have been a very large farm, or a very good one either for regular farming—there was too much sand there and too many outcropping windswept sandstone ledges. But this natural beauty, so peculiar to that section of the country with its numerous summer resorts, all helped to make the farm better for the summer vacation business that was now being done there—the farm land itself didn't greatly matter any more.

Something suddenly popped into sight atop the barn.

"It's a little gray monkey," I excitedly told Red, watching.

"Hi, brother!" he promptly saluted. "Come on down!"

"Pipe down, you dumb cluck!" I gave him a punch, as the monkey ran off shrilly chattering.

"Do you want the whole farm to hear you?   This is no time for funny work."

The cabins, we found, were all in a grove on the east side of the farmhouse.   With their vines and pretty little screened porches and gables they looked like colorful doll houses.   It was plainly seen that they had been built for people who could afford the best.   We got a glimpse of some of the pets, too, mostly cats, but quickly dropped down out of sight when Mrs. Bumblebee herself came out of the farmhouse ringing a dinner bell.

With the farm woman thus located, we felt we ought to get back to the cart without further delay, so back we went through the farm grove to the highway and from there on to the waiting cart.

"D-d-did you see any cats?"   Horse Foot asked us eagerly, when we came running up.

"Sure thing," I told him, jumping in and grabbing the lines to fly off, "and a monkey, too."

"A m-m-monkey?" he repeated.   Then he looked curiously at Red.   "Oh, *you*, huh?"

"I might resent that," Red sniffed superiorly, "if you had a head to hang your cap on like other people, instead of an empty peanut shell."

We had let old Prince take his own time on your first trip in.   But now I kept him at gallop, the branches slapping at us right and left.   Mr. Kelly thought we were crazy, I guess, when we rattled up to where he was working, and tumbled out.

A lanky white-whiskered old man, with a peculiarly prominent mouth and chin, he had gotten down from his ladder chewing and kept on chewing all the time he helped us get our lumber together, though I was pretty sure he hadn't anything in his mouth to chew on. It was just a nervous habit.

"You b'ys are gittin' a heap sight of good lumber fur two dollars," he told us good-naturedly. "That there door and them two windys that you've got are worth that much alone. But it's all right, it's all right," he chewed harder than ever, nodding. "Mrs. Flory Beesaddle and the Woodlawn Bay hotel manager are both tryin' to buy the rest of the building here, but I was told by the New York woman who hired me to demolish it to sell what I could to whoever came along."

We had trouble at the very last finding a safe place on the load for our two windows.

"Let's leave them here and get them later," suggested Red, anxious to get off on the fly again.

"No, no," the carpenter put in quickly, "you better take 'em with you, if you want 'em. Either Mrs. Flory or the hotel manager is liable to buy the rest of the building before the day is over. They've both telegraphed to the New York owner. You prob'ly wouldn't be let to take the windys away after the deal was closed."

The carpenter finally had to come to our aid with the windows, his tongue running further about the trouble between Mrs. Beesaddle and the Woodlawn Bay manager. The cabins, it seems, had taken from the hotel a number of its best-paying patrons and afraid that still more cabins would make the situation worse, the hotel manager had decided to buy up the rest of the partly demolished building as one way of slowing up the cabin owner's building operations.

Our final rush to be off stirred up the old man's suspicions.

"What kind of trickery be you b'ys up to?" he asked sharply, blocking our way. "You can't be in all that hurry jest to get home to dinner."

"We aren't up to any trickery," I told him.

"Well, you act mighty suspicious to me. I still think you're hidin' something."

"Oh, tell him the truth," urged Red, on needles and pins to be off.

Which I did, figuring we hadn't anything to lose by it, the old man listening puzzled at first, and then amused.

"Why," he chuckled, "Mrs. Flory wouldn't 'a' harmed a hair of your heads."

"It wasn't our hair she threatened to work on," shrugged Red. "It was our pants."

"Yes," I followed up, "she threatened to shake us out of them, if she ever caught us in here again."

"But she didn't mean it, b'ys," cackled the old man, more amused than ever. "All the time, I bet, she was laughin' up her sleeve. Why, she's one of the kindest women in the world."

"That's what you think," snorted Red.

"Oh, but I don't jest think it, b'ys, I know it—I've known her fur more'n forty years. Not that I'm doubtin' your story now, or think you're exaggeratin'—I don't mean that—but what you tell me jest don't fit Mrs. Flory at all. I can't fur the life of me figure out why she went at you that way, unless—"

"Unless what?" I asked quickly, as he paused thoughtfully.

"—unless," he finished, "she mistook you fur the Stricker boys from the Woodlawn Bay hotel."

The Stricker boys from the Woodlawn Bay hotel! Could that mean our old enemy, Bid Stricker and his gang?

"Do you mean the Tutter Stricker boys?" I asked Mr. Kelly, staring. "Are they working at the hotel now?"

"That's my understandin'," he waggled. "They started this mornin', I think—anyway I heard yesterday that they were startin' there today, and what little toughies they were. Mrs. Flory hates the hotel manager like p'ison, and if it *was* her idea that you were the Strickers, and that the manager had sent you over here fur lumber, she might have taken that high-handed way of turnin' you back—though she really had no legal right to do it."

"Did she know that the Strickers are working at the hotel?" I asked quickly.

"Yes," the old man waggled, "I told her."

"And is the manager's name Mr. Norning?" I further asked the old man.

"Exactly," he waggled again, chewing in time.

"Then that explains it," I spoke relieved. "She *did* mistake us for the Strickers. It's as plain as day now. But, gosh!—that's the first time in my life that I ever was mistaken for one of that crummy gang."

"Mrs. Flory's goin' to be awful sorry when she hears about it," the old man chewed gravely. "As I tell you, she's kindness itself. Let anyone around here git sick or needy and she's the first one there to help. Oh," the chewer's eyes twinkled, "she likes to boss—I know that! Every time she comes over here she goes 'round sayin', now, Charley, you do this and you do that. But that's jest her way. It's true, too, that she makes people workin' fur her step right along. But that's all right—she pays good, and her help is always used good. Take me here. I'm not workin' fur her directly—at least not yet—but every noon she brings me over a warm dinner."

"Well, when she comes today you tell her about her mistake, will you?" I requested eagerly, as we got ready to drive off.

"Yes," grinned the old man, "I'll tell her. And I bet you git an apology from her—or some kind of a nice present to make up fur it. That's her big-hearted way. She deserves her good fortune with her cabins. As fur that man Norning, I don't like *him* at all—with his smug scheming smile! They say he's French, or somethin' foreign, but he never tells hisself what he is, though he still sticks to his foreign accent and manner. But one thing I *do* know about him, he's aimin' to put Mrs. Flory out of business if he possibly can, either by hook or crook. But I better git washed up now, fur she'll soon be here with my dinner. Maybe I'll know then how she come out. She was expectin' a telygram around noon, she said."

CHAPTER III

MORE TROUBLE

ON THE way out to the highway we met a car coming in.

"I wonder who that is?" I spoke anxiously, as the dapperish little driver got out and started toward us.

"I bet a cookie it's that hotel manager," Red said quickly. "He looks like a foreigner."

"S-s-sure thing it's him," put in Horse Foot. "I can s-s-see the hotel name on the side of his car."

"Good afternoon, boys," the man came up pleasantly, with a fixed smooth smile. "A nice horse you have here," he stopped to pat it.

"Yes, sir," I replied politely.

"Come far?" he then asked.

"From Tutter," I told him, wondering uneasily if he was planning to take the lumber away from us. Having paid for it, I didn't see how he very well could, but certainly he had something tricky up his sleeve.

"I see you've been in here getting some lumber," he looked it over, his sharp black eyes taking in every piece of it.

"Yes, sir," I told him.

"Going to build something yourselves?" he further quizzed.

"Yes, sir," I told him again.

"A cabin?"

"No, sir—a little candy store."

"Oh, young storekeepers, eh?" he pleasantly arched his eyebrows. "That's interesting. It should be a very helpful experience for you, too. This is all lumber from the old hotel, I take it."

"Yes, sir. We just bought it from the carpenter there."

"You—eh—brought along a court order, I presume," came casually, as he walked thoughtfully around the cart.

"A court order?" I followed him around with my eyes. "I don't know what you mean."

"Oh!" his black eyebrows went up again, but gravely this time. "Then you haven't one? That's too bad."

"The lumber's paid for, if that's what you mean," I told him.

He stopped with pretended deep concern.

"I'd dislike very much to see you boys get into trouble," he told us gravely. "That could easily happen to you, though, or to anybody else taking lumber out of here without an official court permit. Just who the rightful owner of the property is has never been established in the courts, though at the present moment a Miss Florence Windmere, of New York City, seems to consider herself the foremost claimant. However, it is the court's duty to protect the other claimants and until the estate has finally been settled nothing here should be removed without a formal court order. Does that clarify the matter for you, boys?"

It did—and it didn't. Having been put out of

here once already, I felt myself that he was just trying to do the same thing, only more trickily.

"How about Mrs. Beesaddle?" I asked him. "She's been taking lumber out of here. Did she have a permit?"

"Unfortunately—no," he pretended concern over that, too, though anybody with any brains at all could see that it was all put on. "Usually a very clever woman and always a most charming one, Mrs. Beesaddle, I'm sorry to say, may find herself in the rather awkward position of having to return every board that she has taken from here."

"Fiddlesticks!" the farm woman here spoke for herself, coming suddenly into sight with a covered lunch basket on her arm. "If you want that lumber, boys," she told us vigorously, "go ahead and take it—he can't stop you, the little windbag!"

The manager's face was cloaked in smiles.

"Oh!" he hid his true feelings under an exclamation of delight. "It is the most charming Mrs. Beesaddle herself! A beautiful June day, my dear Mrs. Beesaddle!"

"It was," she snapped contemptuously, "till I met you. But in the woods, of course, one is liable to meet a snake any time."

Even that didn't ruffle him!

"Coming from so charming a person," he bowed extravagantly, "even a jolly little gibe like that can bring only courteous smiles. So often I have said to myself, 'Oh, the lucky—the *very* lucky Mr. Beesaddle! Not only has he the most charming wife in the community, but also the wittiest.' Mrs. Beesaddle, I bow again to your charming wit."

"If you're putting on that program for my benefit," she told him bluntly, "you might just as well ring down the curtain. I know what you really think of me, and I know what you'd like to do to my cabin business too. Those supposedly polished manners of yours don't deceive me or mislead me in the least. As for you three boys," she turned kindly to us, "I have an apology to make to you. This morning I thought you had come over from his place—that you had been sent over on some kind of trickery of his invention. I learned differently, though, from your friend, the Ellery boy. I'm sorry I was so rude."

"Oh, but my charming lady!" the manager swung in again, with another extravagant bow. "Never, never could that happen. No, never could so charming a lady be rude. It is unthinkable."

Mrs. Beesaddle turned on him with contempt that would have withered any ordinary man on the spot.

"Oh, are you still here? I thought maybe you'd taken the hint and left. Certainly I can't imagine what you're staying for. Miss Florence Windmere surely must have wired you regretfully at the same time she wired me. However, in case she didn't, permit me to very delightedly inform you, Mr. Troublemaker, that in spite of all your efforts to thwart me, the hotel building, as it stands, is mine, to further tear down and use as I see fit. So, defeated again, if you care to get behind your car and let your real feelings show in your face, it is perfectly satisfactory with me. Or if you care to go off fuming in your car, I'm sure no regrets over your departure will be felt here."

That brought some of the manager's true feelings into his swarthy face in spite of himself.

"And did Mis Florence Windmere wire you, too," he asked blandly, "that she had no real right to sell any of the property here? Did she tell you that the estate has never been legally settled since the death, years ago, of her uncle, Gordon Windmere, the hotel builder? Did she tell you further that there are other heirs—the direct descendants of Gordon Windmere—and that the courts are bound to see that the rights of these other heirs are protected till a final settlement is achieved?"

"Bunk!" Mrs. Beesaddle indifferently dismissed the whole matter with a wave of her hand.

"Oh, no, my dear Mrs. Beesaddle," came with evident satisfaction. "It is not, as you say, 'bunk' at all. It is facts, dug up for me by my lawyer. Anything that you or these boys take from here you can be made to bring back. In fact, I shall make it my business to see that it is brought back."

Putting down her basket, Mrs. Beesaddle faced him arms akimbo.

"Mr. Norning, I don't know how much of this nation's early history penetrated the country you came from but, in case you may be poorly posted on the subject, permit me to inform you that the freedom you found here when you got here didn't just happen. It was fought for by a determined group of pioneer fighting men whose descendants are prepared to carry on the fight to preserve it. I can say that authoritatively, for I come of exactly that kind of fighting stock—fighters, all of us! My two great-great-grandfathers fought beside George

Washington throughout the American Revolution; six of my uncles carried arms throughout the Civil War, three on a side; my own husband went off with my cheers to fight in the Spanish-American War an hour after our marriage; and my only child—my boy Tom—gave his life in the recent World War. That in brief, Mr. Norning, is the record of a fighting family. Give us a worthy ideal and if necessary we'll die fighting for it. In this matter I consider myself wholly in the right and to preserve my rights will fight you down to my last dollar, with every ounce of energy I have. Court orders, bah! Failing in every other scheme to thwart me, you come now with this trumped-up threat. Well, it doesn't frighten me, nor will it deter me in the least. If I need more lumber from the old hotel, I'll take it, having authority from Miss Florence Windmere to do so. That's all I have to say to you—you runtish mentally-deficient troublemaker! Good day!"

"Oh, but just a minute, Mrs. Beesaddle!" he stopped her. "Please!"

"I have nothing more to say to you, Mr. Norning."

"But I have something to say to you. I've already offered you six thousand dollars for your farm. I'd advise you to sell, Mrs. Beesaddle."

"I don't intend to sell."

"It might be to your best interests," came blandly.

"Is that a threat?" she stiffened.

"Well," he spoke lightly, but with closely narrowed eyes now, "many unexpected things could happen around here. I'll drop in on you in a week or so. You may be in a more receptive mood then."

"I can tell you right now that I won't, so just save yourself the trip. I wouldn't sell out to *you* for sixty thousand dollars."

"Mrs. Beesaddle," came pleasantly, "I'm going to venture a prophecy."

"I don't care to hear it," she snapped.

"Oh, but I want you to hear it! The prophecy is that before June expires you'll be after me to take over your farm for even less than the six thousand dollars I've offered. That's something for you to think about, my most charming neighbor. Good day!"

They both went off then, one one way and the other the other. Afraid that we'd get into trouble if we kept the lumber, we took it back, getting our money back, and then went off growling ourselves.

CHAPTER IV

OTHER PLANS

"Is THAT you, Jerry?" Mother called pleasantly down the stairs, when I banged in the back door an hour later.

"Nobody else but," I called back, giving my cap a pitch. "What are the chances around here for something good to eat?"

"The chances never were better," Mother accommodatingly flew down and to the range. "I have some meat and potatoes all ready to warm up for you. You'll find some jello in the refrigerator too."

"Hot dog!" I bounded for it. "I'll eat that first."

"You most certainly will not," Mother followed me and firmly took it away before I even got the first bite. "We are still observing a few shreds of table manners around this house, young man. One rule is dessert last, and another is clean hands. So run up to the bathroom and try out that new cake of soap I just put there. It may surprise you what it will do for your hands. Your dinner will be all ready by the time you get back."

Mrs. Rail wheezed in while I was eating, sinking heavily into a chair, fanning her fat face as usual with her apron.

"I suppose, Mrs. Todd," she began the conversation, "that Jerry has been telling you all about his morning's trip."

"Not yet," laughed Mother. "It must have been a very strenuous trip, though, judging from the appetite he brought home. I can imagine how beautiful it was out in the country today—I almost wish I'd gone myself."

"Sammy tried to tell me that the boys saw a real monkey over there," Mrs. Rail went on communicatively. "But I think there's some kind of a joke about it myself."

"No, honest," I told her, between bites. "It was on Mrs. Bumblebee's barn."

"On whose barn?" Mother put in, with a curious amused look at me.

"Mrs. Bumblebee's," I grinned. "That's what Scoop Ellery calls her—he and Peg Shaw are working for her this summer. She's the woman with those cabins that I told you about. Her real name is Mrs. Flora Beesaddle."

"I know her," Mrs. Rail snapped in, like a steel trap going off. "I met her one time at the D.A.R. —the day poor Mrs. Bailey dropped her false teeth out of the second-story window while we were watching the parade. Luckily my Sammy saw the plate falling and caught it—thinking it was a lollipop."

"I suppose it won't be long now," Mother continued politely, "before Sammy and Jerry are in the lollipop business themselves, for I can readily imagine how quickly that candy store will go up."

"Oh!" Mrs. Rail's eyes swelled. "Then you haven't heard, Mrs. Todd?"

"Haven't heard what?" Mother asked quickly.

"There isn't going to be any store.   The boys had their lumber all loaded up, Sammy told me, but had to unload it again."

"What happened, Jerry?" Mother turned to me earnestly.

"Oh," I growled, "Mrs. Beesaddle and a hotel man over there are having trouble over the lumber and we were afraid if we brought any of it home, we'd be drawn into the trouble, too."

"And you had your trip all for nothing!" came sympathetically.   "How disappointing."

"Not to me it isn't," Mrs. Rail again snapped in, beaming.   "I've been half sick ever since I gave in to Sammy about that store.   But now I've set my foot down.   There'll be no store in my yard—at least not in the front yard."

"But you boys can still fix up a little stand, can't you?" Mother suggested, knowing, from all our talk about the proposed store, how disappointed I must be.

"We haven't decided on anything yet," I told her.

Later Red and I got together in his barn, doing a lot of growling at first over our hard luck, but finally getting a lot of fun out of some old beauty parlor equipment that his Aunt Pansy, who had a beauty parlor downtown, had stored there.

"Say, Red," an idea suddenly popped into my head, during our fun, "what do you say if we forget about that candy store and start up a cat and dog beauty parlor here in your barn instead?   How's that for an idea?"

Red grinned all over his impish face.

"Boy, I'd call that an inspiration! But how would you go about beautifying a cat, Jerry?"

"With a real beauty parlor right in your own family," I told him, "you certainly ought to know more about that than me."

"Yes," he laughed, "but we couldn't work on cats like my Aunt Pansy works on her women customers. She gives them mud packs for their complexions, and finger waves and henna rinses. But if we gave a cat a mud pack, the poor animal would be so scared by the time we got the mud peeled off that it never would stop running."

"How about the finger wave you mentioned, and the henna rinse?—whatever that is."

"Don't you know what a henna rinse is, Jerry?"

"No."

"Henna is something you put in the rinse water, and when you rinse your hair in it your hair turns red."

"Is that what makes your hair so red?" I laughed.

"No—mine's stork red," he ran his fingers through it, grinning. "Wherever the red came from it was all there when the storks brought me. But some women do use a henna rinse, Jerry, to redden their hair."

"We could work it easy with a cat, too," I told him. "We could mix up a pailful of rinse and take the cat by the tail and dip it in."

"We'd have to be more careful than that," Red waggled.

"A red cat!" I laughed, picturing how the cat would look when we got it out. "It certainly would be distinctive—especially with a finger wave, too. How do you do that, Red?"

"I don't know exactly, but we can find out easily enough from Aunt Pansy. She pours something on the hair, I think, and then twists it around with her fingers into fancy waves."

"That's two things we could do to a cat to beautify it," I summed up. "What do you think we ought to charge, Red?"

"Ten cents for each operation ought to be about right, don't you think?"

"Can't we think of something else to make it a quarter? Then, if we beautified ten cats a day, we'd make an even two dollars and a half. Boy, I'm beginning to think we could make more money with this kind of a business than a store anyway. With a store we'd have to buy stuff to sell, but with a beauty parlor we could get all the stuff we needed from your Aunt Pansy. But let's get something more besides the finger wave and henna dip."

"Not *dip*, Jerry—henna rinse is the right name for it."

"What's the difference?" I grunted. "It'll be a dip the way we'll do it."

"Let's be professional anyway," he talked big. "Aunt Pansy calls it a henna rinse, so let us call it the same."

"Can you think of anything more that we could do to a cat to beautify it?"

"We might de-flea it," he laughed.

"Suffering snakes!" I squawked. "Does your aunt do *that* to people, too?"

"No," he grinned, "that's my own original idea.

We could build a little bath cabinet, with a hole for the cat to breathe through, and steam its fleas to death over a tea kettle. We could call it our Special Swedish Steam to make it sound big."

I got out a paper and pencil.

"Let's get this down on paper," I went at it in a businesslike way. "Henna Rinse, ten cents; Finger Wave, ten cents; Special Swedish Steam, five cents. There! How about some fancy tail trimming, Red? We ought to get as many things down as we can. With a little practice, we could turn out some pretty nifty tails."

"Put it down then," he nodded. "Fancy Tail Trim, five cents."

"How about toenails?" I asked. "Women have a lot done to their fingernails."

"Sure thing—Toenail Tint and Polish, five cents. Put that down, too."

I looked at him and laughed.

"Shall we really do it, Red?" I asked.

"We'd be chumps not to," he encouraged. "It's going to be a lot more fun than running a candy store."

"What'll we call it?"

"It's your own idea—why not call it Jerry Todd's Beauty Parlor for Cats and Dogs?"

"Something snappier would be better."

"All right! How about *Jerry Todd's Poodle Parlor?*"

"But that just takes in dogs," I objected.

"They sell mops, too, in grocery stores, but the grocer doesn't think he has to print 'groceries and mops' on his window. *Jerry Todd's Poodle Parlor*

is a swell name, I think.   Anybody with good sense
would know from it that we beautified cats, too."

"Well, what'll we do first?" I asked eagerly.
"Get up some fancy advertising signs?—or get some
stuff from your Aunt Pansy and experiment on a
few cats just to see how well we can do it?"

"Maybe we better let the whole thing rest for a
day or two," Red suggested.   "I just happened to
remember that Aunt Pansy and I aren't on speaking
terms right now."

"No?   What's the matter between you and your
aunt?" I asked curiously.

"Oh, some old sweetheart of hers sent her a fancy
basket of wax fruit and I had one of the apples half
eaten up before I discovered what it was.   Aunt
Pansy said I was a little pig.   I told her if I was a
little pig she must be a big pig, for she was my aunt.
Since then she's been looking at me across the dining
table as though I was something the cat had dragged
in.   But her beauty parlor windows downtown are
about due for a washing—my usual job—so she'll
probably sweeten up in a day or two and call on me.
We'll get what we want then, and get some pointers
from her."

"It might be a good plan," I continued thoughtfully, "to find out just about how much cat and dog
beautifying business we could naturally expect from
around here.   We wouldn't be so smart to get
everything fixed up and then find out that there
wasn't as much business to be had here as we
thought."

"Well," Red suggested briskly, "let's go out right
now and find out.   I'll go from door to door on one

side of Main street and you can take the other side."

"And ask the women at the different houses if they want to have their cats beautified, huh?" I quickly fell in with the idea.

"We really aren't in business yet, but we can find out if the women with pet cats would like to have them beautified—at from twenty-five cents to thirty-five cents per cat. But give me your pencil, Jerry, and read off that list—I'll want a copy of it myself to show the women I call on."

When Red finished writing he had a list like this:

JERRY TODD'S BEAUTY PARLOR

(Cat Beautifying Department)

Henna Rinse - - - - - - - - - 10¢
Finger Wave - - - - - - - - - 10¢
Special Swedish Steam - - - - - - 5¢
Fancy Tail Trim - - - - - - - - 5¢
Toenail Tint and Polish - - - - - 5¢

We set out then on opposite sides of the street as he had suggested, calling at every house, but when we got together an hour later we hadn't the name of a single cat owner who was willing to pay even a penny to have her cat beautified, to say nothing of thirty-five cents, the full price. One woman offered us a dime to wash a dog as big as the side of a coal house and ten times as dirty, but we soon saw there wouldn't be enough beautifying business in the cat and dog line to keep the inside of the henna pail wet.

We were laughed off at most houses and at one crabby woman's house we were threatened with arrest if we ever dared to touch the cat belonging there.

So *that* brilliant scheme died, too—at least Red and I thought it was dead when we separated for supper that night, Scoop later calling me up from the pet farm to tell me that he had some kind of an itch on his hands.

"What do you mean?—a cat itch?" I asked him curiously.

"I'd sooner think I got into some poison ivy while chasing that crazy rat terrier around in the woods."

"How are you and Peg getting along?" I further asked.

"Oh, swell—except for my itch. We're sure kept on the jump, but it's fun—we've been getting some nifty tips, too. And, boy, do we ever get the eats over here! Um! Fried chicken almost every meal. They don't give you just a little piece on your plate either, but set down a whole dishful of it to pick from. Mrs. Beesaddle is dandy, too. We like her better every hour. I suppose you fellows are busy as beavers getting your store up."

"There isn't going to be any store," I growled.

"Well, listen!" he came back excitedly, when I completed my account of our hard luck. "Why don't you come over here and get a job? Come on, Jerry! Please! I'll tell Mrs. Beesaddle what a swell worker you are. She'll find a job for you."

"Did you know that Bid Stricker and his gang are working at the Woodlawn Bay hotel now?" I asked him.

"Sure thing. And that's something else, Jerry!" he went on excitedly. "Already Bid has sent word over here that if his gang ever catches our gang in the woods around the old hotel, he's going to turn us inside-out and pack us with sawdust. Don't you see the fun we'll have, Jerry? Come on! Boy, what you and I and Peg couldn't do to that crummy gang! Can we figure on you?"

"I'll have to ask Mother first," I hesitated.

"Oh, she'll let you," Scoop laughed confidently. "But I'll have to go now—someone's buzzing for ice water. See you in the morning, old timer!—I hope!"

CHAPTER V

EXCITING DEVELOPMENTS

I HAD planned to start on my bike for the Beesaddle farm about eight-thirty the following morning,
but to my surprise who should come knocking on the
front door a little past eight but the bustling pet
farm woman herself!

"I'm sorry to burst in on you like this, so early in
the morning," she briskly excused herself to Mother,
when the two had been introduced and we were all
seated in the living room, "but my days are fearfully
crowded and I can't always pick my time."

"That's perfectly all right," Mother assured her
politely. "It's a great pleasure to meet you—and
Jerry here, as you can see, is just about ready to bub-
ble over."

"Yes," I told the visitor quickly, my eyes I guess
dancing, "I was just getting ready to start for your
farm to ask you for a job."

"And I've stopped to offer you a job," she
beamed, looking nothing now like the woman who
had stopped us so severely in the old hotel road.

"Hot dog!" I yipped, bouncing up and down in
my chair. "And will I have a blue uniform like
Howard Ellery's?—with brass buttons on it?"

"That's exactly the uniform you *will* have—for I
had to bring Howard home this morning for treatment. That's one reason why I'm so early, for I

started for town in my car the minute I learned of his condition."

"Treatment?" repeated Mother, her eyes turning anxiously from the visitor to me.   "You mean, he's sick?—already?   After just one day?"

"It's just poison ivy, isn't it?" I quickly asked the farm woman, not wanting Mother to get the frightened idea that the drinking water over there was bad, or anything like that.

"Yes," nodded Mrs. Beesaddle, "he picked up quite a serious case of ivy poisoning in the woods near our place.   But it can't ever happen again to him or to anybody else, for my husband is over there right now digging the poison shrubbery out and burning it.   The Ellery boy will be back in a week or two, so until then I would like to substitute with your boy, Mrs. Todd, if that meets with your approval.   If he waits on my guests attentively, he'll get some nice tips and earn more there in the same length of time than he could any place else.   He'll be well fed, too, and well taken care of, I can assure you of that.   You see, Mrs. Todd," the visitor's motherly face softened, "I once had a boy myself, so I know how boys are and how to handle them.   It is because of the fond memories that I still have of my own boy that I try to draw other boys around me— that is, boys of the right sort.   They make me think of my—my own Tom, as he was at their age.   I lost Tom in the World War and with him it seemed for a time as though I'd lost everything worth while to me—but—what a pretty view you have from your side window," the visitor arose and walked abruptly over.   She wasn't looking through the window, though—she was gently dabbing at her eyes. "Well, Mrs. Todd," she presently turned, with her usual smiling briskness, "do I get your boy or not? I'll have to be hurrying along."

"Jerry's the only child we have," Mother spoke long-faced, touched, I could see, by the other woman's story of her sad loss. "I wouldn't want him to stay away all summer, but if you feel he can do the work you have in mind for him, and if you care to put up with him, I think his father and I can spare him for a few weeks. I might add though—realizing that you will understand—that we aren't so much concerned with what he earns as we are with how well he behaves himself and what he learns."

"Yes," nodded the visitor, "I understand perfectly what you mean and feel safe in promising you that the experience will be a good one for him." With that she popped up to leave. "He'll need several changes of underwear, shirts, socks, handkerchiefs—everything, in fact, except the uniform itself, which I furnish. Possibly you can get his things all ready while I'm down to the bank, as I have a short errand there and would like to get away as soon as I can afterwards. As I say, I hate to rush in on you this way and hurry you with his things, too, but that's just the way my days are throughout the summer—rush, rush, rush! Even then I often have to start a day with things that should have been done the day before. I'm hoping Jerry will be a big help to me. Well, good-by, till I come back for him, Mrs. Todd. You're a grand mother and it's been a great pleasure to meet you."

Red popped in the back door the minute Mrs. Beesaddle popped out the front.

"Lumber trouble?" he asked big-eyed, having recognized the visitor.

"I'm going to work for her," I grinned. "Scoop's home with poison ivy, and I'm going to take his place."

Down slid Red into a chair like a wilted rag.

"Oh, gee!" he made all kinds of unhappy faces. "I wish I could go, too."

I was feeling pretty big.

"With those freckles and that carrot top of yours?" I turned up my nose at him. "Don't be ridiculous. Mrs. Beesaddle wants good-looking bellhops, like Scoop and me and Peg. You couldn't wear a blue uniform with brass buttons. They'd think it was just another monkey running around over there. No, Red," I swaggered around, "you better stay home and help mamma with the dishes and get Aunt Pansy's beauty parlor windows washed up nice and neat. That's more your kind of work. I'll give you a ring now and then to tell you about our fun, or drop you a postcard."

"Boy, would I ever like to paste you!" he glowered.

"Tut, tut!" I waved him off lordly. "Don't step out of your place now, infant. Remember you're just an inexperienced child."

That got him after me, fists flying, and getting me down in the hall he went at me like a little fury. The racket finally brought Mother flying down the stairs, her arms filled with shirts and underwear.

"Please, please!" she went at us impatiently, Red finally getting up and slouching off.

"I'm going home," he growled, banging the screen door behind him.

I quickly followed him out.

"I was just fooling, Red," I told him. "Gosh, I'd give anything myself if you could get a job over there, too! And maybe soon there will be enough work for one more. If there is, you can bet your last penny that you'll be the one we plug for."

"You always were lucky," he sat down miserably on the back porch steps. "Oh, gee, I wish I could have a little luck like you once in a while! I don't know what I'll do around here without you, Jerry."

"You still have Horse Foot," I told him, with a straight face.

"That dumb goose egg!" he exploded. "Huh! I won't waste any time on him. I'd sooner play with the girls than with him."

Around the corner of the house then clattered Horse Foot himself, popeyed and breathless.

"Mrs. B-b-bumblebee's in town, Jerry," he panted. "I j-j-just saw her in the bank."

"I know she's in town," I told him. "She just brought Scoop home—he's all plastered up with poison ivy and I'm going to take his place. She's coming back for me as soon as Mother gets my clothes packed."

"H-h-how soon'll that be?" he asked quickly, his eyes jumping excitedly.

"Oh, in ten minutes or so, I guess."

He started for home on the gallop.

"T-t-tell her to wait for me, too," he yelled, as he started to go around the corner of the house.

"Hey!" I took after him. "Hey, wait a minute! Nobody said anything about you going. Hey, stop!"

But when I got to the corner he was completely out of sight.

"Do you suppose he's really gone home to pack up?" I stared at Red.

"He's dumb enough to," grunted Red. "And nervy enough, too."

"Well, it isn't any of my business," I dismissed the matter with a shrug. "Mrs. Beesaddle certainly won't take him with her if she doesn't want him."

"Jerry!" Mother impatiently called from an upper window. "Go in and answer the phone. Goodness me, can't you be of any help to me at all— with me hurrying to get your clothes ready!"

I found Peg on the wire.

"Is Mrs. Beesaddle there, Jerry?" he asked quickly.

"No—but she's coming back here in a few minutes. Why? Has anything happened over there?"

"There's an important telegram here for her. Do you want to take it down?"

"Sure thing—read it to me, and I'll give it to her when she gets here."

This is what I wrote down:

Mrs. Flora Beesaddle,
Back-to-the-farm Cabin Colony,
Tutter, Illinois.

Will arrive this evening with De Puster ken-
nel prize apricot poodles stop must have large
airy cabin and special attendant and quarters
for poodles stop am grooming poodles for ex-
hibition at international London show in July
stop attendant must have knowledge of canine
beauty parlor practices stop results of July ex-
hibition of utmost importance stop will not ob-
ject to your pet farm getting favorable publicity
from my visit if everything is satisfactory.

(SIGNED)

Mrs. Hetty Hinds, 3rd.

"Did you get it all?" Peg asked at the finish.

"I think so.   But what does all the stop, stop,
stop mean?"

"Oh, that's just the same as a period," he explained quickly.   "The telegraph operator explained that to me when I took down the wire from
him.   Wherever you see a stop, that means the end
of a sentence.   I don't know who this Mrs. Hetty
Hinds the third is, or what she means by all that big
poodle talk, but she seems to think herself that she's
pretty important—so I thought I better let Mrs.
Beesaddle know about the telegram as soon as possible.   She told me she was going around to see you.
Scoop and I have been pulling hard for you, Jerry.
I hope she hires you."

"She already has," I told him happily.

"Hot dog!   For the whole summer?"

"Mother wouldn't let me hire out for the whole summer, but I'm to stay till Scoop gets back, and maybe longer."

"Boy, I hope someone gets here pretty quick! I'm run ragged—with that blamed buzzer going all the time. Honest, Jerry, you'd think these people here hadn't any arms or legs, the amount of waiting-on that they require. It's get me some ice water and get me some ginger ale and get me a newspaper and get me some matches and get my dog a biscuit and get me, get me, get me! So the sooner you get here to help, the better for me."

"Red would like to get in there, too," I told Peg, when he finally weakly ran down. "He's all cut up because I'm leaving this morning."

"Well, why doesn't he apply for that poodle attendant job?" laughed Peg. "The poodle woman wants someone with beauty parlor experience, and certainly he must have picked up some experience while hanging around that beauty parlor of his aunt's."

Beauty parlor experience! A poodle attendant! And we had been talking about starting a poodle parlor!

"Hello!" Peg jiggled the hook at his end. "Are you still there, Jerry?"

"Sure thing," I told him excitedly. "I was just thinking of something. You see, Red and I were talking just yesterday afternoon about starting a beauty parlor for cats and dogs in his barn. We were going to call it a poodle parlor, too. So when you just made that suggestion!—and mentioned a beauty parlor and everything!—well, gosh, Peg, you

—you almost took my breath away! It was almost as though you knew what we had been talking about and were trying to help us from your end."

"It does look like a set-up?" he laughed oddly.

"Almost perfect—if you ask me. We decided it wouldn't work here in town, but it's exactly what you need over there. A poodle parlor! Will Red ever be surprised when he hears that we're going to have one after all—and possibly with him running it! I'll tell Mrs. Beesaddle all about our scheme as soon as she gets here," I wound up excitedly. "Gee, I hope she does hire Red! Wouldn't it be swell if she hired all four of us?"

"Bid Stricker just phoned over again that he's going to get me tonight, rain or shine, so the more of you that turn up here before dark the better for me. Otherwise I'll have to fight the gang all alone, I guess. Boy, they can't bluff me out!"

"Well, you're sure of me," I told him, tickled pink that I was going to be in it myself.

"And m-m-me, too," put in Horse Foot, who had come in while I was talking and now stood listening.

"I'll have to go now, Jerry," Peg told me hurriedly, "for the old buzzer's going again."

Hanging up, I went at Horse Foot sharply.

"What did you mean by that 'and me' stuff?" I demanded.

"I'm goin, t-t-too," he beamed.

"Listen, nervy!—you've got entirely too much crust. Wait till someone asks you to go."

"S-s-she did, Jerry," his eyes danced.

"Who?" I began to stare. "Mrs. Beesaddle?"

"S-s-sure thing," he bobbed his head. "I called

her up at the bank and said could I g-g-get a job like Jerry Todd, and she said s-s-sure—to get my clothes and meet her here."

And Red had called him a goose egg! Boy, there wasn't any "goose" about him—unless he was the "goose" that got the early worm!

"Aren't you g-g-glad I'm going, Jerry?" he beamed.

"But you can't go," I yelled at him, on Red's side. "We want Red first. He was in the gang first and he should come first."

"I'm h-h-hired," Horse Foot strutted. "I'm g-g-going to be head poodle tender."

"Did Mrs. Beesaddle tell you that?" I further stared.

"S-s-sure thing."

"And you're sure she said poodle tender, and not just dog tender?"

"No, she s-s-said poodle tender."

"Then she must know about that telegram already," I quickly thought it out. "The telegraph operator must have heard she was in town and looked her up to tell her about it."

"I t-t-think he did, Jerry, from what she said."

"But she certainly was loony if she hired *you* for a poodle tender," I fired my scowl back at him.

"S-s-she said she remembered me," he further beamed proudly.

"I don't know how she could ever forget you!" I sneered. "But listen, Horse Foot," I changed to a nice persuasive wheedle, "why don't you let Red have first chance? Please! You wouldn't like to take care of a mess of poodles anyway—they're snippy looking things! Why don't you wait till we can get you a better job over there?—taking care of some nice big Saint Bernards? For Saint Bernards are heroes. They're more your type, Horse Foot —and not poodles! Oof! No, you don't want that job."

"B-b-boloney!" he motioned me off. "I do, t-t-too, want it."

"If you'll wait," I went on persuasively, "I'll give you the two dollars we were going to buy lumber with."

"Nope," he bit off.

"And I'll throw in my air gun," I further offered. "Nope."

"And a pair of roller skates," I piled it up. "Nope."

"Well, then," I asked desperately, "what will you take?"

"I'm h-h-hired, and I'm going," he said flatly.

CHAPTER VI

AT THE PET FARM

A CAR drove up noisily in front and stopped.

"H-h-here she is, Jerry," Horse Foot scooted excitedly to the front door with the big suitcase that he had packed his clothes in.

I still was sore at him for not giving up his pet farm job to Red, but had given up arguing about it then, hoping that when I got him over there I could make him change his mind, or that an opening would turn up for Red, too.

Tangling with his ungainly suitcase, Horse Foot went down full length in the hall, the hall tree tumbling noisily down on top of him.

"O-o-ouch!" he got up rubbing his head.

"Goodness me!" Mother came flying. "I thought the whole front of the house was coming down. Did you say that Mrs. Beesaddle is here?"

"S-s-sure thing," Horse Foot excitedly started off again with his suitcase. "S-s-she just drove up."

"Oh, go dig out your eyes!" I told him, after a quick look out. "That isn't Mrs. Beesaddle's car— it's a grocery truck going to your house."

"But w-w-why doesn't she come?" he sat down on his suitcase disappointedly, still rubbing his head. "We've been w-w-waiting for her for an hour."

"Yes," Mother looked up the street, "I thought

myself that she'd be here long before this from the
way she talked.   It's after nine o'clock."

There was another sharp ring from the phone.

"Maybe that's her now," I jumped to answer it.

But it wasn't—it was Peg Shaw again, this time
with the startling news that Mrs. Beesaddle had
been seriously injured in Tutter when a heavy truck
had collided with her car and was now in the hospital.

"Where did it happen?" I asked Peg, stunned.

"Between your house and the bank.   It's queer
you didn't hear about it before us, being so close.
Still I guess it isn't so queer either, for as soon as
they found her name in her purse they phoned here
—and it couldn't have happened more than twenty
minutes ago."

"Boy, that's bad, isn't it?—and right at the beginning of her summer season, too."

"It's hard to tell yet what the cabin renters will
do, even if we all pitch in together to keep the place
going," Peg continued.   "But I guess that's all we
can do.   I figured on a summer's job here and
would still like to make it a summer's job, if I can.
So if you want to take a chance with me, Jerry,
jump on your bike and come on over."

"I'll start right away," I promised him.

"Maybe you better bring Red, too," he advised,
"for we'll need all the help we can get with Mrs.
Beesaddle away."

"How about Horse Foot?" I asked.   "Shall I
bring him, too?"

"I'm not so crazy about him.   Can't you get
some bigger boy?—who can do more?"

"Mrs. Beesaddle hired him, he says. She was going to let him tend those poodles that are coming."

"Well, bring him along then," Peg consented. "I don't think much of her choice, though."

"I don't either," I agreed. "I'd certainly hate to trust him with any valuable poodles of mine."

"That's another thing, Jerry!—the cabins are all full. What are we going to do with that poodle woman when she gets here tonight? From her telegram you can see that she expects the best of everything."

"What do you think Mrs. Beesaddle would have done?" I gave the problem right back to him.

"I don't know. I haven't been here long enough to get the swing of things. But maybe Myrtle will know. She's been here since the first of May. I'll ask her."

"And who's Myrtle?" I asked.

"Myrtle Bean," he gave the full name. "She does all the work in the cabins, and the dishwashing. There's a lady cook here, too, from Chicago. With you fellows, we'll have plenty of help, but as I say I don't know whether we can satisfy the cabin renters or not. They think that Mrs. Beesaddle is the only one who can wait on them understandingly. But we'll try and get things organized as best we can when you get here, and make a try at it. I've got to go now. Hurry over, Jerry! So-long!"

Hanging up, I wheeled to Horse Foot.

"We'll have to go over on our bikes," I told him quickly. "So snap into it. See if you can't make a smaller bundle of your clothes and forget about that young bungalow that you've got 'em in now—you'll never get that on your bike unless you hitch a trailer to it.   I'm going over now and get Red, for he's going, too.   Be ready to start from here in five minutes."

"B-b-but what's the matter with Mrs. Bumblebee?" he stared blankly.   "Isn't s-s-she coming for us?"

"Yes," Mother put in anxiously, "what happened to her, Jerry?   I couldn't quite gather from your talk with Peg."

"She's in the hospital," I relayed quickly.   "She had a bad smashup downtown, and Peg wants the three of us to come over on our bikes just as soon as we can to help him.   Will you hunt up some ropes for me, Mother?—I'll have to tie my clothes on the handlebars.   I'm going for Red now, but I'll be back in just a minute or two."

Mother had my clothes all tied on when I got back and with a hurried good-by and with Red and Horse Foot after me, I took off down the river road as tight as I could go.   Horse Foot soon fell behind, but Red puffing kept up with me.   Crossing the river bridge, as on the day before, we turned to the left, passing the old Windmere road finally and finishing up at about ten-thirty in the Beesaddle farmyard.

When I say farmyard, though, don't imagine that I mean the usual bare farmyard, with corn cribs and barns built unattractively around it and wagons and machinery scattered about in it.   There was a barn here, as mentioned before, and corn cribs and other necessary farm buildings, too, but there was no sign of them from in front. Fast growing bushes and trees, such as poplars and willows, had been planted in what had been the old farmyard to hide the buildings and help with the new beautifying scheme that Mrs. Beesaddle had ambitiously worked out for her summer business.

We had come in under a flowering vine-covered arch from which neatly hung the farm's name-board, and from which, on both sides, extended a low-trimmed hedge. Inside, on both sides of the hard-surfaced winding drive, were wide closely-cropped lawns, with artistic white benches scattered about in the shade, and in the sun so many contrasting flowers that you could almost have imagined that it was a plant nursery of some kind, instead of a summer cabin colony—as the cabins themselves, farther back and to the right, were completely concealed from the highway by more trees and vines. There was even a fountain there, dancing in the sunlight with birds all around it. Boy, it was one of the prettiest spots I ever had been in!

Peg caught sight of us from the vine-covered farmhouse and tore out.

"Hi, there, general!" Red saluted impishly, as our big chum came up in his neat brass-buttoned uniform.

One of several children and of a poor family, Peg has been in my gang from the time it was first organized. He has been a mighty helpful member of the gang, too, with his big muscles and dogged grit. He never picks a fight, but woe to the boy anywhere near his own size who picks on him! In our battles

with the Strickers, it was always Peg who did the
most to send the enemy off squealing.

Just now he sure did look like a million dollars in
that nifty uniform of his, with his broad shoulders
and sturdy frame.

"So you decided to leave Horse Foot home after
all, huh?" he asked us quickly.

"No—we just out-pedaled him," I explained.
"He'll be along in another hour or two, if he doesn't
get lost. But where are all the people around
here, and the pets?" I looked around curiously.
"All I can see is a couple of cats down that walk."

"Don't worry," he growled, "you'll see plenty of
pets before you get through here. I wish though
that Horse Foot had kept up with you, as I was going to send him over to cabin number six—the
woman there wants someone to read to her pet
Pekingese, Whoopee. How about you, Red? It's
just easy stuff like Little Red Riding Hood. Do
you want to take a crack at it for your first job?"

"Oh, you're fooling!" Red looked silly.

"Fooling nothing!" snorted Peg. "The woman
who owns the dog is rich enough to hire it read to,
so it has to be read to. If it wasn't read to—or if
anybody here was to hint that reading a dog to sleep
was silly—off the owner would go in a huff with her
fat pocketbook. Go ahead and try it, Red. You
might as well start with that as something else. I'll
look up a uniform for you later. And for Pete's
sake act like you thought it was the biggest treat in
the world to read a dog to sleep—particularly that
dog. Even beg to come back and do it again—
you'll get a quarter tip from its flattered owner if

you do; or if you'll gently kiss it good-by before you tiptoe out, you'll get a half dollar. We love our pets around here!"

"I think I'll take the quarter," grimaced Red. "But what cabin is it?" he looked back through the bushes. "And what's the woman's name?"

"Mrs. Helene Blakeley. The cabins are all down that winding drive. The first one is number one and the one at the far end of the drive is number eight. She's in number six."

"Number six, huh? O.K."

"But, listen!" Peg enjoined. "When you go down there don't clatter past the other cabins and wake up any cats or step on one. I tell you again that every pet here has to be carried around on a silver platter—if you get what I mean. That's the way Mrs. Beesaddle keeps the people here and makes her money. Wrecking her car that way and going to the hospital is going to cost plenty, fellows, so remember that everything you do here now to keep the guests contented and keep the money coming in is going to help Mrs. Beesaddle a lot—as well as ourselves."

"But tell me—do I have to get in any gestures when I read?" grinned Red. "Or do I just sit there and read?"

"Try some gestures," Peg grinned in return, "but keep an eagle eye on Mrs. Blakeley. If you see she likes it, give her some more—it'll all mean dimes and quarters in your pocket. While Mrs. Beesaddle is making her profit out of the cabin renters, I don't see why we shouldn't scheme a little bit and make all we can, too."

"Boy," laughed Red, never more full of nonsense than now, "that Pekingese will think I'm Julius Caesar delivering his own funeral oration—or was it Mark Antony? You know what I mean: 'Friends, Romans, countrymen, lend me your ears— I had to send my own to the laundry.'"

"You've got the right idea," Peg patted Red on the back. "Well, go to it, boy! I'll take charge of your clothes here. We have a little cabin all our own down there by the barn in that cluster of poplars—the dormitory, Mrs. Beesaddle calls it. The bell will ring when dinner's ready. We eat in the kitchen with the rest of the help. Jerry, I'll take you over to the dormitory now so that you can wash up. We have a neat little washstand there, with a swell chest of drawers for our clothes and a separate bed for each. I like it because it's off by itself— we can have all kinds of fun there nights if we don't get too noisy."

"Is there room there for my bike, too?" I asked.

"Yes, bring it along, Jerry, and I'll take Red's. Come on!"

CHAPTER VII

GETTING INTRODUCED

PEG took me past the farmhouse, with its small front porch and larger side dining porch, and then to the left through a fringe of poplars to the mentioned dormitory behind.

"Well, here we are, Jerry," he gestured hospitably, when we were inside, bikes and all. "Pick out any drawer you want to over there, except the top one, and any of the single beds, except the one at that end—for that's mine."

"Then I'll take the second bed," I told him quickly, getting my bundle of clothes off to put away. "I'll take the second drawer, too. That'll be easy to remember."

Peg at the same time quickly got the other bundle of clothes off.

"We'll give Red the third drawer down," he planned, "and let Scoop and Horse Foot fight for the last two, if Scoop ever gets back. Boy, he sure was a sight when he left here this morning! His fingers and ears were puffed up like auto tires."

"Mrs. Beesaddle said I was to have his uniform," I told Peg quickly, eager to get into it and get to work.

"Yes, it's over there in that closet," he pointed. "There's one for Red, too, and a whole row of white waiters' jackets. The boys who worked here last summer had to wait on the table, too, but Myrtle's been doing it so far this summer—though we may have to help her from now on."

"What will Scoop wear when he gets back?" I asked.   "One of the white jackets?"

"Yes, and we'll put Horse Foot into one before that poodle woman gets here tonight, for we'll want him to look as much like a beauty parlor operator as possible.   She may not stay though when she finds out that she'll have to sleep in the farmhouse.   But that's all I can do for her—till one of the cabins is vacated."

"You talk like you're running the place," I laughed.

"I am."

"But where's Mr. Beesaddle?   Don't you let him have any say at all?"

"I thought I told you—he's in town with his wife."

Getting my shirt off I looked around the long narrow room for the mentioned lavatory, finding behind a partition at the south end hot and cold showers as well.   The neatly made beds were set crosswise of the room, all in a row, half on one side of the screened door, which opened on the east side, and half on the other.   There were small screened windows on all sides, too, for ventilation, and at the north end a small fireplace had been provided for use in cool spring and fall weather.

"Well, what do you think of the old shebang?" Peg followed me around with his eyes, his own broad grin showing what he thought of it himself.

"It's swell," I told him enthusiastically.

"Yes," he glowed, "and are the beds ever swell! Um-um! We get clean sheets every day just like the guests—only we have to make up the beds ourselves. They all have to be made up just like you see them, too—Mrs. Beesaddle's orders!—with the sheets turned back just so-so and the pillows right in the middle, without a crease. Yesterday Scoop and I got our orders not to lay on the beds in the daytime either—though I don't know when anybody'd ever get a chance around here to do that with that crazy buzzer going all the time."

"I've heard so much about that buzzer, I'm getting kind of anxious to see it," I laughed, running the washbasin full and getting my face in.

"You'll see plenty of the buzzer before you get through here," Peg predicted, watching me from the washroom door. "Myrtle's tending it now, though I told her to disregard any buzzes except from Mrs. Clarabel Piper in number one. Boy, when we get a buzz from her we jump and I don't mean maybe— for can she jaw!"

"What kind of a pet has she got?" I asked curiously, wanting to get lined up as quickly as possible.

"Did you say *a* pet?" Peg snorted. "Listen, short weight, she's got two canaries named Dicky and Dotty, two goldfish without names, two big angora cats named Merry and Diggs, one Pomeranian —that's a dog—named Toodles, and a husband."

"Does he get petted too?" I grinned through the towel, feeling good to get the dust from my hurried bike trip washed off.

"Petted?" Peg snorted again. "You wouldn't think so if you heard her going for him, though he takes it easy enough himself.   He's funny—the way he answers her.   You see, their money all came from her side of the house so she figures that makes her the boss.   Instead of using his name, she calls herself Mrs. Clarabel Piper; so he calls himself Mr. Clarabel Piper.   Usually they're gone all day in their car scouring the country for antique furniture. Wait till you see the stuff they've got packed in their cabin—you'll think it's a curiosity shop."

Getting quickly into my nifty blue uniform, all cleaned up now and combed up, I took a proud look at myself in the mirror over the fireplace.

"Boy, are the cats and dogs around here ever going to get a treat now!" I set the little gold-trimmed cap that went with the suit jauntily on the side of my head.

Peg watched grinning.

"Myrtle was asking me what you looked like.   I hope she falls in love with you and gives me a rest. She sure is eager!—and plenty odd, too!   She has some of the funniest ideas!"

"How old is she?" I asked curiously, with another proud look at myself.

"Oh, about your age—or maybe a year older. Last night she wanted me to walk up and down the cabin road with her in the moonlight, but I told her my feet hurt.   She'll probably be after you tonight."

"Who is she?" I asked further.   "Some relative of Mrs. Beesaddle's?—or some farm girl from around here?"

"I haven't been enough interested in her to inquire.   But if you can tear yourself away from that mirror, big and handsome, let's get going.   This isn't just a dress parade, you know.   There's work to be done here."

Some dog-eared books on the mantel caught my eye at the last moment.   They were all boys' books, some just plain adventure stories but some with such purposeful titles as, "Good Boys Make Good Men" and "Boys Are Men in the Making."   I soberly took one down, finding as I had suspected that the books had all belonged to the son that Mrs. Beesaddle had lost in the war.   And she had put the books here for other boys, to please them and possibly help in guiding them!   She sure was a grand noble woman all right.   Until then I had thought mostly of what I was going to earn there, and the fun I might have.   But now I felt glad all over in knowing that what I would do there would help her, too. Banged up as she was and with the crafty Woodlawn Bay hotel manager scheming to undo her, she certainly deserved all the help I could give her, or the other boys either.

"You can look at those books tonight," Peg told me impatiently.   "Come on."

When we were outside he locked the door, hiding the key under a flat rock near-by.

"That's so the Strickers won't get in and mess up our things," he explained to me, as we started back through the fringing poplars.

I had forgotten all about the Strickers, and Bid Stricker's cocky threats!

"Have any of them been over here yet?" I asked Peg eagerly.

"No," he shook his head, "but they phoned that

they're coming tonight.   They think I'm all alone,
I guess."

"Boy, will we fix them!" I giggled, eager for the
fun.

"Yes, but we haven't time to gab about that now.
We'll settle them when the time comes."

"I wonder how Red's getting along with
Whoopee?" I laughed, as we came out in sight of
the colorful separated cabins set so prettily on their
winding drive and paralleling stone walk.

"Shall we go over and listen for a few minutes?"
Peg suggested, grinning.

"Sure, let's," I eagerly endorsed.   "I'm anxious
to see more of the pets over there."

A woman's voice came to us sharply from the first
cabin as we came up.

"I tell you again, his name is *not* Jiggs.   It's
Diggs.   I've told you that a hundred times."

"There, there, mamma!" came in a drawling pla-
cating voice from a raw-boned man comfortably
rocking on the front porch.   "Remember your
blood pressure.   Don't get excited now.   You
wouldn't want to miss seeing that rare old Colonial
what-a-ma-gig this afternoon that you've got spotted
in Tutter.   So don't wear yourself down, mamma."

"It *isn't* a what-a-ma-gig," came the sharp exas-
perated correction, as the speaker bustled around
inside.   "It's a whatnot.   You know that as well
as I do—but you just call it a what-a-ma-gig to be-
little my interest in antiques."

The man started clapping vigorously.

"And what's that for?" the woman demanded.

"Why," came meekly, "I thought that was the

end of your act, mamma, and I was giving you a little applause."

"Jimpson Piper! Are you making fun of me?—after all I've done for you all these years? Haven't you any gratitude at all?"

"Now, now, mamma, remember your blood pressure!" the man rocked comfortably. "Tut, tut! There isn't room enough for you to faint in there anyway—you might bump your head on some of your what-a-ma-gigs and leave a dent in 'em. Compose yourself now, mamma."

A short stubbed woman came into sight in the door.

"Who is it pays all the bills around here? It's *me!*"

"Ho-hum!" the man yawned.

"Who provides the home? It's *me!*"

"Ho-hum!"

"Who buys the motor cars? It's *me!*"

"Come, come, mamma!—you're wearing an awful groove in that record."

"Who is it buys all your clothes? It's *me!*"

"And who wears the pants?" was injected slyly.

"Yes, and who wears the—Jimpson Piper! Are you trying to insinuate, on top of belittling my interest in antiques and poking fun at me, that I'm bossy and domineering? Just because I *have* to pay the bills—if they're ever paid!—is it necessary for you to hint that you're henpecked?"

The man jumped up and cowered behind his chair, almost twice as big as she was.

"Stop!" he panted, as though cornered. "Stop

where you are, mamma! If you hit me with that
cupboard door again I'll scream for help."

"Oh, you big goose!" the woman burst into a
laugh. "But probably it's just as well that one of
us does have a sense of humor. Sometimes I do
scold too much, I guess. But you know, Jimpson,
that I don't mean it. I couldn't possibly get along
without you. But quit your nonsense now and give
that buzzer a press—I want to find out how Mrs.
Beesaddle is. I may call on her this afternoon
when I'm in Tutter, if she can receive visitors."

Peg took me on, chuckling.

"And that," said he, as he hurriedly steered me
through some bushes to the next cabin, "is Mrs.
Clarabel Piper and Mr. Clarabel Piper in a characteristic little home scene."

"O, Romeo, Romeo! Wherefore art thou,
Romeo?" came to us from the second cabin, in a
dramatic emotional feminine voice.

"Is that the actress with the parrot?" I asked
Peg quickly, as we stopped.

"Yes, but who told you about her?" he quizzed in
return.

"Scoop. He said she was going to be in a play
here."

"That was the talk, before Mrs. Beesaddle got
hurt—she was going to let them fix up a stage in the
barn—but I don't know whether there'll be a play
now or not. Anyway, I don't know how they could
put on *that* play—Romeo and Juliet—for the only
two men here are both too old and stiff to climb up
into a balcony. Captain Otis Danglers, in num-

ber five, even has a peg leg. That would be a hot one, wouldn't it?—a peg-legged Romeo!"

"What is he, an army captain?" I asked.

"No, he's an old seaman—with a pet monkey. But let's stop here, Jerry, and I'll introduce you to the actress—if you're going to work here she ought to know who you are."

"Robbers!" furiously rasped the parrot on the screened porch when Peg tapped on the door. "Cut-throats and robbers! Call out the guard!"

A tall willowy finely-featured but overly-painted woman glided girlishly into sight, a book in hand.

"Yes?" she inquired pleasantly.

"This is one of our new bellboys, Miss Martow," Peg introduced, when we were inside. "His name is Jerry Todd. I'm showing him around so that he can be of greater service. And this, Jerry," Peg pointed to the ruffled glowering parrot, "is Mr. Tweedle-de-dum. Has he had his morning cracker, Miss Martow?"

"Oh, yes, thank you!" beamed the actress. "It was most kind of you to stop unsolicited to inquire. And I'm pleased to meet you, Jerry. I'm sure that we'll find you very helpful around here."

Peg kicked me slyly.

"I guess that's what you call a beautiful parrot, huh, Jerry?" he beamed at it.

"Oh, boy!" I laid it on. "I'll tell the world."

"I hadn't thought of him as being so particularly beautiful," cooed the actress, her wrinkles showing through her make-up, "but he has a most remark-able mind for a bird. He often repeats whole lines from my plays."

"I'd like to hear him," Peg spoke eagerly.

"Did you hear that, Mr. Tweedle-de-dum?" the actress purred to the parrot. "These nice boys would like to hear you recite."

"Oh, piffle!" the parrot clawed its perch gloweringly.

"Come now, Mr. Tweedle-de-dum! Begin: O, Romeo, Romeo!—Let's hear you say the rest of it."

"Fum-a-diddle!" the parrot rasped again, as though completely disgusted.

"He evidently isn't in a reciting mood right now, Miss Martow," beamed Peg. "But I know that he can do it all right—for he's smart and pretty, too. Any time you want anything for him just give a buzz. It's a pleasure to do things for him, and for you."

That got out a big box of chocolates.

"Oh, take some more," the girlishly-dressed actress urged.

So we took some more—in fact, we kept on taking more till there weren't any more to take!

Peg almost lost a finger, though, when he held out one of the chocolates to the parrot.

"Naughty, naughty!" the bird's owner reproved gently.

"He likes to play, doesn't he?" Peg passed it off lightly, with a final loving look at the bird.

But outside he looked his finger over growlingly.

"Boy, would I ever like to give that feathered neck a nice expert twist! But it so happens that we don't do what we want to do around here!—we do what'll best please the pets' owners, and smile about it. So if he ever slashes at you, Jerry, instead of kicking his back porch off, just take it with a grin. That's the third slash I've had from him.   But let's see if Vixen's on the job."

"Who is Vixen?" I inquired.

"The Scottish terrier in the next cabin.   He belongs to a Mrs. Trudy Dartling, who is entertaining her young niece, Miss Irene Garton.   Miss Garton just came this morning on the bus.   But wait a minute!—I see Myrtle waving to me from the farmhouse.   I suppose it's that buzz from Mrs. Clarabel.   You wait here, Jerry.   I think I can get back in a minute or two, and then I'll show you the rest of the way around."

CHAPTER VIII

AN EXCITING MORNING

It took Peg longer than he thought, so finally I sat down under a tree, a young woman in the next cabin looking out at me curiously as I fooled around with a couple of cats there.

"Did you really enjoy it, Aunty?" she then asked the other woman in the cabin.

"Why, of course I did, Irene," came in an older affectionate voice. "I thought it was one of the best children's plays that I ever had heard on the radio. It was so human—so real."

"I wish, Aunty, that I had been brought up in an orphanage," came impulsively. "I'd like to know just how orphaned children live."

"But why do you feel that you have to write solely about little orphans, Irene? Don't you like to write adult plays?"

"I seem able to write so much more convincingly about children. If I ever do succeed in getting a serial on the air—as I have been striving so hard to do for the past year—I'm sure it'll be a children's story, and probably a story of orphans, too. If only I knew better how they actually live and work and think—what their real griefs are, their hopes and joys."

"Well, why don't you visit an orphanage some time," came the practical suggestion.

"Oh, but I have, Aunty!—I've been to several of them in and about the city. But that doesn't give me the insight that I want. I just see things as those in charge want me to see them. And it's hard for me to put myself in the place of an underprivileged child while you have showered me with so much all my own life. Aunty dear, I doubt if you fully realize yourself what a truly wonderful daddy and mother you've been to me—for you are the only parent I ever have known."

"I could scarcely have done less for you, Irene— my own brother's child."

"You loved daddy very dearly, didn't you, Aunty?"

"We loved each other very dearly, dear. His loss, and the almost immediately following loss of your dear mother, almost overwhelmed me. But all the joy of living and of service came back with you. It seems but a few months ago that you were given to me, a mere squirming armful!"

"And without a penny!—just a squawking little responsibility, financial and otherwise! Daddy couldn't have had your head for business, Aunty."

"He was just unfortunate in his investments. But of course all that I have will be yours some day. That is why I feel it is so foolish for you to remain in the stifling city, with your work, when we could have such a wonderfully pleasant summer here together. Won't you stay with me, Irene? Please!"

"Oh, Aunty!—no!—you precious! I must get back to my newspaper work on the late afternoon bus. I just ran down for a few hours to make sure that you and Vixen were happily settled for the summer. You see, Aunty," came gravely and earnestly, "I am quite determined to make my own way in life hereafter—really, I feel that I should, and I want to. I'll admit that my newspaper work isn't anything sensational, but it does pay the butcher and baker, leaving me the time I need for my more important endeavor—radio writing."

"But, Irene," came persuasively, "where could you find a more ideal writing spot than here?—with the beautiful country all around you, and all the woodland quiet that you could possibly need but a few steps away. You admit that your newspaper work isn't important. So why give it time that you might better spend on your more promising work? Vixen and I adore it here—he has such a jolly exciting time chasing mice in the barn and romping and digging so freely. But if you feel that the pets here would be distracting, I'll gladly cancel my arrangements and get a more secluded place in Tutter."

"Oh, Aunty!—stop! Do you imagine for one instant that I'd drag you away from this paradise of pets? Don't I know how you looked forward all winter to getting back?—yes, you and Vixen both! The pets might be a trifle distracting at first—but, as you say, there are plenty of quiet writing spots near-by. I'd love it, too! But really I can't possibly stay, as you suggest. Why, in no time at all, with the heavy meals you have here, I'd be so lazy I'd forget that I ever had had any worthy ambitions. And really, Aunty, I do want to succeed in radio writing, if I can."

"What do the radio editors tell you about your work now, Irene?"

"Some say nice things, and some not so nice. But the fact that I've had a few plays broadcast is encouragement to me to go on to the bigger things that I have in mind. It's just a matter of development—and opportunities. Oh, Aunty, why *didn't* you chuck me into an orphanage? Think what it would mean to me now. Can't you hear the radio announcer saying: 'And now, boys and girls, gather close to your radio, it's time for the daily installment of Miss Irene Garton's famous story of Wilma the Waif!—brought to you by Blah-Blah Breakfast Buns—the breakfast that cleans your teeth for you, gets all your schoolwork for you, and gives you more muscle to fight each other with—and of course a hand-crocheted bicycle seat with each box top.' There you are, Aunty!" the girl's excitement ran laughingly to a peak. "Five weekly plays at a hundred dollars apiece! I have the plays all worked out in my mind. All I need is someone to put them on the air and pay me the hundred dollars apiece."

"Bow-wow-wow-wow!" the mentioned dog came in then.

"Stop it, Vixen," came the low sharp reproof.

"Who is he barking at, Aunty?"

"One of the guests in number five. He has a peg leg and something about it always starts Vixen to barking whenever he passes."

"Why, Aunty!" came breathlessly. "I know that man."

"Captain Danglers?"

"I never heard his name, but I'm sure it's the man I mean. I met him under rather odd circumstances. I'm quite excited to find him here.

Oh, if only—But tell me, how long has he been here?"

"He came with a monkey about two weeks ago. But how could you possibly know him, Irene? He's more than double your age."

"I'll tell you later, Aunty—but tell me first, did anybody come with him, or on the same day?"

"I really don't recall, Irene."

"Well, then, tell me more about the people here —maybe that will help me. How many cabins are there and who occupies them?"

"I told you about the actress on one side of me and the Cookbook Woman on the other side."

"Yes?" came breathlessly.

"There's a married couple in number one—a Mr. and Mrs. Piper. The Captain who just passed occupies number five. There's a Mrs. Helene Blakeley in number six. There's still another woman in number seven, I think. And the final cabin is occupied by—"

The voice dropped below my hearing there. But whatever was said in a low voice seemed to strangely excite the girl.

"Then you're going to stay?" came happily from the older woman.

"Yes, Aunty. I want to find out the truth. And if it *is* her and I'm successful—Oh, Aunty, Aunty! Won't it be wonderful?"

Peg popped up then, tapping on the door of number three and introducing me to the older woman there—a rather frail faded little body who in turn brought out her niece, with instructions to have a permanent place prepared for her in the dining porch.

The girl herself sure was a smart-looker all right, with her natty clothes and pretty face and ways. What I had just overheard made me particularly curious about her, too—and about the occupant of number eight.

The Cookbook Woman in cabin four had gone off with her seventeen cats to the river to catch them some minnows, so I didn't get to see her till later, but got a slightly different story from Peg as to why she had given her pets such odd names. It seems that she had gotten together enough tested cooking recipes to fill a book, printing it then with her own money and now getting a big income from it. It was after her own original recipes that she had named her pet cats. In a way they were a living testimonial to her success.

Captain Danglers, too, was out. I caught another glimpse of his little monkey though, on the rooftop, as Peg and I passed down the winding walk to number six, where Red inside was giving Little Red Riding Hood the workout of a lifetime. Boy, was he getting in the emphasis and the gestures! Of course, we couldn't actually see him, but we could readily imagine what was going on in there from the way it sounded. Here's where he was in the story when we got there:

(Gruff voice) "The better to see-e-e you, my chiild!"

(Sweet voice) "Grandma, what big ears you have!"

(Gruff voice) "The better to hear you, my chi-ild."

(Sweet voice) "Grandma, what big arms you have!"

(Gruff voice) "The better to hug-g you, my chi-ild!"

(Sweet voice) "But, Grandma, what big teeth you have!"

(Furious gruff voice) "The better to eat you up with!"

"Bow-wow-wow-wow!" a snooty bark broke in on the climax.

"I'm afraid, Donald, that you make the story too dramatic," came a woman's slightly sharp voice from the front porch, as Peg and I stood back grinning together, knowing pretty well what was going on in poor Red's mind right then. "As I explained to you when you started, Whoopee is very sensitive to dramatic inflections. Suppose you start over again and strike a more tranquil lullabyish tone."

"You mean—the same story again?" Red's voice sagged. "I've read it three times already."

"Please!" came frigidly. "That is Whoopee's favorite story. Begin at the beginning, please."

"Oh, all right!" Red growled in his characteristic way.

"The big sap!" Peg grunted in my ear. "What difference does it make to him how many times he reads it? He'll never get any tips that way."

"I can hardly blame him," I replied. "It does look awfully silly—reading to a dog. I know how he feels."

"Of course it's silly," Peg admitted without argument. "A lot of the stuff we have to do around here is silly. But there's no use getting superior about it—if we expect to hold our jobs and keep the place going. We're getting paid for it. If we're smart we can double our pay in tips, too. So what's the sense of getting muley about it, like Red? Don't *you* do it, Jerry. You do as I tell you now. I'll get after him again, too."

Taking me up to the porch then, Peg briefly introduced me to the Pekingese's owner, a tall severe-looking woman with fixed sharp eyes and a set jaw, who sat in a rocker jabbing with a crochet hook. Hearing us, Red took time out for a peek, like a hunted cat, but got back to his job in a jiffy at a sharp cough from the crocheter.

There was a great stir in number seven, the fat panting moon-faced woman there telling us resentfully, when we stopped, that she was getting out just as quickly as she could throw her clothes into her suitcases and get into her car out in front. Not another hour, she flew around, her face getting redder every minute from the unaccustomed exertion, would she stay in a place where the service was so indifferently poor as it was there.

"You can get me my bill right away," she snapped at Peg. "And if there's anything marked down for Reginald's breakfast, you can cross it off. That's mainly what decided me to leave—for here it is almost noon and the poor famished darling hasn't had a bite yet. And where's my mail? Where's my morning newspaper? Where are the stamps I ordered yesterday?—I told you plainly enough that

I'd need them the first thing this morning. But where are they? Where's the boy who was going to wash my car, too? My bed hasn't even been made up, or anything here tidied up! When I press the buzzer what do I get?—nothing! And you expect pay for such lack of service as this! Well, you can get your pay after this from others more gullible —I'm leaving."

This was the owner of the rat terrier that Scoop had had to chase into the near-by woods with such disastrous results to himself. The dog itself was now playing with a rubber ball on the tumbled bed.

"I know, Miss Greene, that the service has been awfully poor this morning," Peg excused guiltily. "But you know, I just came yesterday. And with Mrs. Beesaddle in the hospital, and Mr. Beesaddle gone, too, I've been at my wit's end. I tried to do the best I could alone. You won't have any complaint from now on, though, for this is another bellboy— Jerry Todd. We have still another one to help, too. So you better let me unpack your things again," came persuasively, "and then I'll see that Reginald gets the swellest breakfast he ever had. I'll get your stamps, mail and everything else, too."

"Reginald and I will get what we need at the Woodlawn Bay hotel," the woman snapped again. "That's where we're going, as I noticed a new sign there yesterday stating that they're now giving special attention to guests with pets. So hurry up and get me my bill, as I said. I'm anxious to get away from here."

The two big airedales in the last cabin set up a fearful barking outside then as the Cookbook Woman

from the river passed by with her procession of cats.
Frightened, the scattered cats took to the trees and
bushes, the two galloping airedales hot after them.
One of the scooting popeyed cats got up Miss
Greene's screen door and to save it she opened the
door to let it in. Before she could coax the cat
down though, in bounded the two airedales themselves.

All primed for a fight and probably having been
squinting sideways for days at snooty little Reginald,
they took after him now in lieu of the cats. Boy,
did that four-legged pedigreed peanut ever hoof it
around that cabin, over the bed and under it, the
covers flying, and through the opened suitcases.
Never had I heard such ki-yiing and barking in all
my life—yes, and screaming, too, for don't imagine
for one instant that Miss Greene intended to stand
there mute and let the intruders chase her poor little
Reginald clear out of his hide—and right on his own
premises, too! I guess not! She was in the mad
whirl almost as much as the three dogs themselves,
trying to grab the particular tail that belonged to
her as the three whizzed by, and finally getting after
the whole lot with a broom. At the height of the
racket, the airedales' elderly owner came running in
from next door to help quiet her pets and probably
apologize for the disturbance they had caused, but
almost immediately ran out again, hiding her face
with her hands as her large green goggles were sent
flying at a misdirected swish of the broom.

Peg finally got the airedales out and back on their
own porch, at the same time returning the peculiar
goggles to their owner, who reached with a wrin-

kled hand for them through her door crack without
otherwise showing herself.

"Thank you," she said simply, the door then clos-
ing.

"Who is she?" I asked Peg, bubbling with curiosity about her now, as we waited near by for a call
from the terrier woman to come and get her packed
luggage.

"That's what a lot of people around here would
like to know, Jerry," Peg laughed. "She's listed in
the register as Mrs. Hannah Topple—but that's
probably just a phoney name."

It was getting more interesting every minute!

"But what makes you think that she's living here
under a phoney name?" I went after all the details
I could get.

"Why, from her actions—like you just saw her
now. The other guests call her the Hideaway
Woman. About the only time she shows herself,
even in her goggles, is at dusk when she walks out
with her dogs. Myrtle thinks she's some kind of
royalty hiding here. But you like mysteries," came
the added laugh. "Why don't you take a whirl at
this one, Jerry, in your spare time—if you ever do
have any spart time around here!"

"That's exactly what I am going to do," I decided.

Already I knew that there was some kind of a
connection between the Hideaway Woman, as she
was called, and the peg-legged Captain, and also a
further connection between the Captain and the young
radio writer. Of course, it was none of my business
—nobody had asked me to go snooping into their
private affairs, nor was there any apparent reason

why I should. But it was too much for me to have a mystery like that under my nose without getting into it.

"Don't do anything, Jerry, to annoy her or drive her off," Peg then enjoined. "I'm sorry this Greene woman is going off angry, and certainly don't want to lose any more of our guests. I don't like the idea of her going over to the Woodlawn Bay hotel either —it'll just give the manager there another chance to knock us, which is what he does every chance he gets, anyway. But, gosh, it wasn't my fault this morning! I did everything I could—the woman in there might at least have been a little more reasonable."

"Anyway," I told him, "we're going to have an empty cabin now for the poodle woman."

"Yes—I'll have Myrtle get it ready just as soon as this woman leaves," came businesslike.

This mention of the poodle woman brought Horse Foot into mind.

"How long have I been here?" I asked Peg quickly.

"Oh, about an hour, I guess."

"Then Horse Foot should have been here long before this. I wonder what happened to him?"

"Why worry about him?" Peg tossed the matter off unconcerned. "We won't need him till tonight —when the poodle woman gets here. But there's Miss Greene calling now! When we get her luggage into the car we'll ride on the running board to the farmhouse and give her her bill. Come on, Jerry."

CHAPTER IX

MYRTLEOVA THE GREAT!

I WAS ready for real business now having been clear around the place, so after the terrier woman had driven off in the direction of the near-by hotel, Peg further hurried me into the farmhouse, the old living room of which had been made over into an office, and put me on duty at the buzzer-board near the registration desk.

"All you have to do is to sit here on this bench and keep your ears open," he told me briskly. "If you hear a buzz, look up at the board—for every time a button is pressed in any of the cabins there's a buzz here. One buzz means, 'Bring me some ice water,' and two buzzes means, 'Come and find out what I want.' "

"But how'll I know which cabin to go to?" I asked.

"By the lights on the board. There's one for each cabin."

"Oh, sure, I catch on now. If I hear a buzz and see number two light on, I'll know it's the actress, huh?"

"Bright boy! You got the idea right off. You hear the buzz; you see the light; you service the call; and when you come back you trip the light like this —see? Then it's ready to come on again."

"Do we take turns answering the calls?" I asked.

"If there's three of us on the bench, the one who

comes in from a call takes the outside and works in,"
Peg explained. "That makes it fair for all. I like
Miss Martow's calls best myself—she's always so
nice, though she doesn't tip as generously as some of
the others. One, three and eight are the best tip-
pers."

A loud harsh voice here reached us from the
kitchen, where the noonday meal was being rushed
to completion. We could hear someone out there
sobbing, too.

"I wonder what's wrong out there?" Peg
pricked up his ears, worried. Then he started snif-
ing. "I can smell something burning. Gosh, do
you suppose they've burned the dinner? I believe
they have for a fact. Oh, of all the rotten luck!
It would have to happen just when we were most
anxious to have everything go off smoothly."

A girl my size ran in from the kitchen then, her
face buried in her hands.

"Let go of my arm," she sobbed, when Peg
stopped her. "I'm going to my room. I'm not
going to help that old black witch another minute.
For that's exactly what she is—an old black witch.
And I wish my Fairy Caterpillar would come along
and spin a web around her and change her into a
bat—a nasty old black bat!"

"But you can't go to your room now, Myrtle,"
Peg tried to reason with her, still hanging to her.
"Gosh, it'll soon be time to ring the dinner bell.
And don't cry that way! You'll make yourself
look like the dickens. Remember, you've got to
wait on table in a few minutes."

"I just wish my Fairy Caterpillar *would* change

her into a bat," came spitefully, between sobs. "I do, I do, I do! For she's nothing but an old cross-patch."

"Well, let's not get excited about the bat and caterpillar," Peg grunted dryly. "Here, sit down in this chair and tell me what you're crying about. Suffering cats! You'll be a sight for the guests! Oh, stop it, Myrtle!" he shook her crossly. "You're just putting that on. I know you! I haven't worked with you a whole day for nothing."

The girl's hands, I had noticed, were red and coarse, as though she had had to scrub floors and wash dishes all her life. She looked sort of tousled, too, with her heavy head of curly auburn hair tumbling down in her face. She wasn't the neat tidy kind of a girl at all—more the ragamuffin type. And when I saw her face!—oh, oh! With her freckles and pug nose she was anything but a beauty. She even had green eyes!

She was looking coyly into Peg's face now.

"You're so-o kind," she stretched it out dramatically, with an appealing little quiver in her voice. "You're the only one here who understands me."

"Oh, rats!" he growled, flushing. "Don't start getting sentimental again. If you aren't the limit! What did you do out there in the kitchen anyway? Tell me."

"I'll tell you vat it is," a scowling swarthy woman spoke with an unpleasant foreign accent from the kitchen door, arms akimbo. "Nothing she is but a stupid lazy little do-nothing—of more hindrance to me than help."

That brought another violent outburst from the girl.

"You see!" she sobbed. "She hates me! She hates me!"

"Oh, pipe down," Peg told her roughly. "What is it, Mrs. Switzer?" he then anxiously asked the scowling cook. "Gosh, whatever it is, let's get it straightened out in a hurry if we can, for it's almost dinner time. What happened between you two anyway?"

"The gravy—I say to her, now you vatch it while I go by the milk house for the cream for the dessert. Not do I say to her, you *make* the gravy—I yust say, keep it moving with the spoon. Yust little t'ings like that have I ever asked her to do—but never right or careful does she do them. To Mrs. Beesaddle I say it once, I say it twice, I say it a hundred times—*she is no good*. Mrs. Beesaddle kindly say—oh, in time she will learn. But now I say, no, no, *no!*"

"Just a minute," Peg swung in dizzily. "What happened to the gravy—that's what I'm interested in."

The cook drew herself up with a gesture of finality.

"There is no gravy! Out I had to throw it—all of it. So burned was it that not even a starving dog would more than sniff at it."

Poor Peg almost turned white.

"No gravy!" he squawked aghast, his eyes jumping to the clock over the desk. "Gosh, we've simply got to have gravy. Can't you make some more out of milk, or something?"

"A whole panful of fine chicken gravy I had," the cook further suffered over the loss. "So careful I make it, so there vill be not one lump in it, for that number one lady who scolds so, she say, I von't eat it, I von't eat it—it's lumpy. Today I say there vill be not one single lump in it. Then out goes it all! Ugh!"

"But you haven't answered me," Peg desperately kept at her. "Can't you make more gravy?"

"No," came the flat refusal. "After this meal I am through. Yust so soon as I get packed up after dinner, I go back by the bus to my Chicago."

"Oh, no, no!" cried Peg, ready to tear his hair. "Please, Mrs. Switzer. We'll raise your pay. We'll get you another girl. We'll do anything—but please, please don't walk out on us now."

"When the bus it go by at two-thirty," the cook laid down finally, "back I go by my Chicago. I no like it here anyway. Such foolishness with dogs and pussycats! Now I leave before all the vork it fall onto me, with Mrs. Beesaddle away. Yes," came conclusively, the woman going off, "this afternoon I leave."

"Now we are in a mess," Peg paced distracted, when the muttering cook was back banging in the kitchen. "No gravy for dinner—thanks to you, lazybones! And even worse, probably no supper tonight unless we get it ourselves. What are we going to do, Jerry?" he turned despairingly to me.

"Why don't you ask me?" the girl looked up impishly, with not the slightest trace of grief in her funny little face now.

Peg wheeled on her savagely.

"You better keep still if you know what's good for you!" he yelled at her. "I'm not going to ask you anything. You're too dumb."

The girl got up and danced around on her toes. "Yes, but I made you think I was really crying," she looked archly at Peg over her shoulder as she pirouetted around the room. "So you see, I'm not so dumb after all. I'm very clever at acting. And some day I'm going to be a great dancer like Pavlova. My Fairy Caterpillar is going to bring me a dress of gold, with a rare old lace bodice and little tinkling gold bells down the sides. Then I'll dance for kings and queens. I won't have to watch a nasty old gravy pan then, or be scowled at by silly boys. I'll be the toast of the Continent. Myrtleova the Great!"

I got Peg's eyes, open-mouthed.

"What's the matter with her?" I gurgled. "Did something just hit her on the head?"

Myrtleova the Great! And all that silly talk about her Fairy Caterpillar! It sounded plenty cuckoo to me—especially coming from a girl as plain as she was. Girls like that didn't ever get to be famous dancers. It took pretty girls for that.

"This is the Dying Swan," she told us, going into a crazy whirlwind dance, her arms flapping like a bird's wings. "This is what I was practicing in the kitchen when the gravy burned."

Peg finally caught her and flopped her back into the chair, mad enough at her now to almost wring her neck.

"Listen, dumb expression!" he grated, his eyes glinting. "We know your brains are all in your

feet—you don't have to demonstrate. But suppose
for the minute you just let that swan of yours do a
little of its own dying while you help us figure out,
if you can, what we're going to do here."

"Did you like it?" the girl eagerly turned up her
shining green eyes to him. "Did it really make you
think of a dying swan?"

"Oh, Myrtle!" he sank helplessly into another
chair, ready to give up. "What's the matter with
you anyway? Don't you realize the mess we're in
and what'll happen here in another few hours if
we're left without a cook? The guests will all
leave. Think how Mrs. Beesaddle will feel when
she hears that. It'll ruin her. Don't you want to
help her? Gosh, it almost looks as though you
don't! You're certainly the oddest girl I ever
bumped into."

"It's my temperament," she gave herself an air of
superiority. "All great stage artists are tempera-
mental."

Red tumbled in then whistling with a fifty-cent tip,
the Pekingese having finally succumbed to Little
Red Riding Hood.

"When do we eat?" he asked hungrily.

"Say, Red!" Peg jumped at him eagerly. "Do
you think you could wait on table this noon?—I
mean, take the soup around on a tray, and stuff like
that?"

"Sure thing," came confidently. "But what kind
of soup is it? Boy, I hope it's noodle soup, for do
I love noodle soup. I'll stick my thumb in every
bowl. Um-m!"

"Well, listen!" Peg was all business now.

"THIS IS THE DYING SWAN," SHE TOLD US.

"And you too, Jerry. Just forget about the buzzer-board for the time being and get into a couple of those white jackets I showed you in the dormitory. Get Red into that last uniform, too—but leave your brass-buttoned coats off—just wear the white jackets. You're going to be the waiters this noon, for I'm through with that nitwit over there! Huh! This afternoon I'll see if I can get another cook from somewhere around here. I'll get another girl, too —one with some brains in her head instead of in her feet! But let's first do our level best with the dinner, to make that go off well. We'll go after the other stuff later."

There were three sharp buzzes from number eight.

"Mrs. Topple wants her lunch brought to her," the girl jumped up.

"Well, we'll take care of Mrs. Topple and everybody else," Peg told her meanly. "You can go out in the orchard and finish killing off that swan if you want to. We don't want you around here. And this afternoon when the cook goes you go, too."

"I will not!" the girl faced him with flashing eyes. "Mrs. Beesaddle hired me for the summer and for the summer I'm going to stay. I'm going to take Mrs. Topple's lunch to her, too, as that's one of my regular duties. Furthermore, having been here the longest, I'll give you to understand that I'm the boss and intend to give the orders hereafter."

"Then I quit," Peg started hot-headedly to stripping off his jacket. "If I have to take orders from a rattleheaded nitwit like you, I'm through."

"Very well," the girl told him, with her head up

like a queen. "I'll figure up your pay right after lunch. As for the rest of you boys, you can completely disregard that order about the jackets. *I'm* waiting on table today as usual. Are you the Todd boy?" she asked me.

"Yes, ma'am," I gulped it out, hardly knowing what to expect from her.

"Well, you can tend the buzzer as before," she motioned me back to the bellboy bench. "And what's your name?" she demanded of Red.

"Little Red Riding Hood," he simpered, with one finger in his mouth. "What's yours?—Jennie the Giant Killer?"

"No, it's Myrtleova the Great," Peg sneered in.

"*You* can go out in the kitchen and help the cook," the girl told Red authoritatively, ignoring Peg.

"I'm not going to wash any dishes," Red rebelled, in his squawking way.

"You'll do exactly what I tell you to do," the girl fired back at him. "And if I get any sass from you I'll box your ears. Now get along, you mouthy little monkey-face, and make yourself useful as well as homely."

"The girl's crazy!" squealed Red, clawing his hair, his eyes popping.

"Git," she told him, shooing him toward the kitchen.

The change in her had set Peg to grinning all over his broad face. Full of spunk himself, he was quick to admire it in others.

"Hurray!" he danced hilariously. "I knew we could put it over, with a little cooperation. Who cares who the boss is around here, just so we make good. You give the orders, Myrtleova old hoofer, and we'll see that they're carried out. But for Pete's sake don't get any more of those Dying Swan ideas when you're carrying the soup tray around and pour soup down somebody's neck."

"After lunch," the girl told him, her eyes gleaming like emeralds, "I'll dance it all for you. It's wonderful! It's my own interpretation, too. It will bring all Europe to my feet. Oh, I can almost hear the plaudits of the multitudes now—when I'm Myrtleova the Great!—the toast of the Continent!"

"I think the toast will go better tomorrow morning for breakfast," Peg grinned, in his sturdy sensible way. "But that's all right, Myrtleova! When we have time I'll be glad to see you dance—and the other fellows will, too. But there's other work to be done now, so let's all get going—everybody."

The number eight light was still on.

"How about that three-buzz call?" I asked Peg, when the girl had run off to finish setting the tables in the adjoining dining porch, and get ready for the bell.

"Say, that's right—I'd forgotten all about it. Come on to the kitchen and I'll get a tray ready for you—for Myrtle can't stop to take it over now even if it has been her regular job."

The Hideaway Woman, it was then explained to me, had arranged specially to have all her meals served to her in her cabin, which explained the three-buzz call. That was her signal that she was ready for her lunch and wanted it brought over right away.

Myrtle came by as I was starting out.

"What do I do?" I asked her. "Rap at the door?"

"Just set the tray on the little porch stand there," I was told. "She'll take it in herself after you're gone and give you four buzzes when she wants you to come for it."

"Say, Myrtle," I eagerly held her a little longer, to find out all I could before I started, "you were here when she came, weren't you?"

"Yes."

"Did she come with Captain Danglers?"

"No."

"Well, what reason did she give for wanting to have her meals served in her cabin?"

"I don't know as she gave a reason. She just wrote and said she wanted the most secluded cabin we had, with special meal service, and one evening later on she walked in with her dogs and goggles and took possession."

"She walked in, huh?" I studied that point. "Then she must be someone from around here."

"Or someone brought here in a car and let out down the road," Myrtle gave another idea.

"That's right, too," I conceded quickly. "Have you ever seen her without her goggles?"

"No."

"They were knocked off this morning in number seven, but she had her hands over her face almost before we realized what had happened. She's an old woman, though—I could tell that. She must be some well-known woman, too, or she wouldn't be so fearful of recognition. I got a tip that Captain Danglers knows who she is. I think that young woman that came this morning knows, too. It looks to me as though the old woman either is here spying on the Captain, or the Captain is spying on her— with the girl possibly spying on both. Do you think Mrs. Beesaddle knows who the old woman really is?"

"No, but I do," came unexpectedly.

"You do?" I almost dropped the tray. "Who is she?"

"The Duchess of Caterpillar Land. My own Fairy Caterpillar told me so one night in a dream."

The Duchess of Caterpillar Land! She sure was an odd little girl and with all of her plainness an unusually appealing one, too.

But what made her say such queer things? Was it just a case of too much imagination? Or was it genius of some sort trying to express itself?

I was to get the truth later on. When it came out it made me pretty long-faced, too. The poor kid! No wonder her hands were coarse and calloused—and don't get the idea either that work piled on her by Mrs. Beesaddle had made them that way. They were that way when she came.

CHAPTER X

GROWING MYSTERY

"WHAT! No gravy?" Mrs. Clarabel congealed in her chair, when the guests were all in for lunch, two and three at a table. "Did you hear me, Myrtle?" followed sharply. "I said I haven't any gravy on my potatoes. Mr. Piper hasn't any gravy either."

"I'm awfully sorry but the gravy was burned to-day, ma'am," explained Myrtle, fluttering around in a fancy little white apron and cap that showed up her rough red hands more than ever.

"No gravy? Humph! A fine state of affairs. Have you found out yet when Mrs. Beesaddle will be back? I certainly hope it's soon—if this is an example of the inefficiency that is likely to prevail here during her absence."

"We're expecting a call from the hospital in a few minutes, ma'am."

"Well, take my plate away and bring me another one without potatoes. I simply cannot eat potatoes without gravy. Take Mr Piper's plate away, too."

"Oh, that's all right, mamma!" Mr. Clarabel quickly spoke for himself. "I like mashed potatoes with butter on."

"Only children eat buttered mashed potatoes," he was told frigidly. "Myrtle, away with our plates—both of them. You heard me."

Myrtle audibly giggled as Mr. Clarabel hastily gobbled into his mashed potatoes before they were whisked off.

"And don't tuck your napkin into your vest," his wife further went at him across their little table. "Put it down in your lap. The people around here will think you were brought up in a zoo. *Jimpson!* Don't you see that actress eyeing you over there? She's been all over Europe. Show her your manners. Don't make me ashamed of you."

"Yes, Maggie," he mumbled obediently, but with rebellion beginning to gleam in the back of his eyes.

"What did you say?" snapped his wife, drawing the amused attention of the other diners nearest her.

"I said, yes, mamma," he meekly mumbled again, his eyes down.

Peg and I in white jackets were tiptoeing around to see that everybody had water and to help with the removal of the empty dishes, as Mrs. Beesaddle herself always had done when she was there.

"Why did he call her Maggie?" I asked Peg, as we went out to the kitchen together to fill our water bottles.

"Did you hear that, too?" he laughed, hungrily looking over the pieces of cream-topped strawberry pie that had been set out in a row to be served later with the coffee. "He was giving her a dig because she's so bossy."

"But I don't get the 'Maggie' part yet," I puzzled.

"Why, after 'Maggie and Jiggs' in the funny papers, of course. He knows he's henpecked. That cat Diggs of theirs—he calls it Jiggs, too. Boy, does that get the old girl up on her ear!"

Red was licking out the whipped-cream bowl, dabs of cream all over his face.

"Oh, boy!" he smacked, in his glory. "And look at all the soup we've got left, fellows! I'm going to eat mine out of the dishpan."

Myrtle came flying in.

"That old cross-patch of a Mrs. Clarabel! Her chicken is too brown now and there's too much dressing on her salad. The bread's too heavy, too. I almost wish she would leave."

"I don't think she means anything by it," Peg gave his thoughtful opinion. "It's just a habit with her. But where's Mrs. Switzer? She hasn't pulled out already, has she?"

"Everything's dished up," shrugged Myrtle, with a quick look around. "And she always did leave all the cleaning-up to me, though from the way she ran me down this morning you'd think that all I ever did around here was to sit and twiddle my thumbs."

"I knew the truth," grunted Peg, with an approving look at her. "I've seen plenty since I've been here. I *was* mad at you though for burning that gravy—just when we didn't want it burned. But how much do we owe the cook?" he got down to business. "Do you know, Myrtle?"

"Yes—but don't bother me about it now," the girl flew off.

At twelve-thirty the hospital phoned that x-ray photographs of the patient had disclosed a serious hip injury, which probably would keep her in the hospital for several weeks at least.

Which was the news that Peg gravely relayed to

the expectant guests at the conclusion of their noon-day meal.

"Mr. Beesaddle himself ought to be back here before night," Peg continued above the sympathetic murmur that went around. "With his help we're going to keep the farm going. Our cook is leaving today, too—I might just as well tell you all the bad news in a lump and get it over with!—but we'll have another cook here before night. So if you'll just be a little bit patient with us and overlook a few things like the burned gravy today, I'm sure that in a day or two you'll find everything almost as satisfactory as when Mrs. Beesaddle had charge herself. We're just hired help—Myrtle, I mean, and us three boys—but we like Mrs. Beesaddle and we're going to do everything in our power to help her."

"Which is a fine noble stand," came impulsively from the actress, with a look at us that made us feel good. Then she gracefully arose, looking around at the others. "With these boys taking this splendid stand, friends, I feel the very least we can do—with Mrs. Beesaddle's misfortune at heart ourselves—is to be patient and considerate till the organization here is perfected. We can even help a little bit, too! We've had so much done for us, I feel it would be nice—yes, even exciting!—to do a few things for ourselves. One time I was snowed in at a house party, without servants, and we had great fun doing things for ourselves. Of course," she concluded, feeling that maybe she had said too much and flushing slightly over it, "that is just my own suggestion."

Captain Danglers jumped onto his peg leg as she gracefully sat down.

"And shiver my timbers!—who could make a finer suggestion?" he boomed in his characteristic gruff blunt way, his pointed gray mustaches and heavy gray eyebrows working savagely. "I even say myself, why bother to get another cook at all? *I* can cook! All true sons of the sea can cook!— and I'll lay to that. Furthermore how about our charming associate here?" he turned gallantly to the warm-faced elderly Cookbook Woman. "I understand that Miss Cane here has compiled what is authoritatively considered one of the best cookbooks in the country. So with professional talent like that to draw on, why should we go outside for a cook? Miss Cane, what is your opinion on that?"

"Oh, but I couldn't possibly cook for so many," came in a flushed panic from the modest little owner of the seventeen cookbook cats.

"Thunderation!" further brusquely boomed the Captain, his sharp black eyes snapping. "Who said anything about you doing all the cooking? My good lady, that wasn't my idea at all. Shiver my timbers—*no!* But you could give us some occasional pointers, eh?—about some of your fancy dishes? That wouldn't be so much of a task, would it?"

"Oh, no, that would be a pleasure," came relieved.

Up popped dumpy little Mrs. Clarabel.

"Just a minute!" she rapped authoritatively for attention with her fork butt.

"Yes, my friends," elaborately gestured the Captain, "I give you now the charming Mrs. Clarabel

Piper, who wishes to add her own suggestions. Mrs. Piper, the floor is yours."

Mr. Clarabel applauded vigorously.

"Speech! Speech!" he cried.

"Oh, keep still, you big goose!" his flushed wife tried to kill him with a look, as a politely restrained titter went around. Then getting herself in hand she added: "I simply arose to ask you a question, Captain Danglers."

"Madam, to answer a question of yours will be an honor. Proceed."

"You just said something to Miss Cane about her giving *us* cooking suggestions—and I want to know just who you mean by *us*. Certainly I have no intention myself of turning cook here in hot weather like this. I came here to rest, not to exhaust myself over a hot cook stove. *I* make the motion that we hire a new cook immediately. All those in favor say—"

"Stop! Stop!" boomed the Captain, thumping with his peg leg. "My dear misguided lady, give me a chance to finish. I was going to suggest that we men gallantly take over the cooking—with possibly a little help from Miss Cane—until Mrs. Bee-saddle is able to make other arrangements."

"Splendid!" Mr. Clarabel approved enthusiastically. "The men will put on the food and the ladies will put on the weight. Splendid, I say!"

"Then I have your hearty support, Matey?" asked the Captain.

"To the very last dimpled dumpling, Skipper."

But Mrs. Clarabel wasn't backed into a hole yet by any means!

"Just a minute! Just a minute!" she rapped again for attention. "Captain Danglers," she then proceeded dryly, "I have no way of knowing what your own culinary accomplishments are, but of Mr. Piper himself I can truthfully say this: He couldn't fry an egg if you heated the pan for him and dumped the egg in."

The look of smoldering defiance that I had detected in Mr. Clarabel's eyes came right out in the open then.

"Now, mamma," he drawled above the laughter that her sharp belittling statement had stirred up, "you know very well that I prepare all the meals at home, while you're gallivanting around after those Colonial what-a-ma-gigs of yours. Who is it coaxes the eyes out of the elusive potatoes?—It's *me!*" he gestured in imitation of his wife that morning. "Who is it rounds up the rebellious prunes and de-wrinkles them in the saucepan?—it's *me!*" he gestured again. "Who is it grapples with the haughty onion and subdues it to soup in the soup kettle?—it's *me!* Who is it—"

"Oh, Jimpson Piper!—will you hush!" his scarlet-faced wife finally got in.

But Mr. Clarabel was going too good to stop!

"No, I won't hush!" he pounded the table, in further pattern of his wife. "I *can* cook and you know it, too, and if Captain Danglers still wants me to help him I'm going to help him. I guess I still have a few rights of my own, even if I am just Mr. Clarabel Piper. Just because you pay the bills and wear the pants—"

Everybody was roaring now and seeing just one

way out of the embarrassing situation Mrs. Clarabel took it, running off into a silly titter herself.

"My husband is such a joker," she beamed around,
when quiet had been restored. "And of course to
keep up with him, I have to have my own occasional
little joke, too, about his cooking. Tee-hee-hee!
You know how husbands and wives are, friends!
Jimpson is simply *marvelous* with a frying pan. Oh,
dear, yes! Are you listening, Jimpson dear? You
see, I'm complimenting you now. With you and the
gallant Captain working together, I'm sure we'll
have some *marvelous* meals. But what about us
ladies? Are we simply going to sit here idle and
let you two unselfish noble-spirited men assume all
responsibility for the cooking? Oh, no!—no, indeed! Ladies, *we* are going to help, too. Miss
Cane, you and I are going to plan the meals—that's
to be *our* little responsibility. Miss Martow, you
and I will see to the ordering. And, Mrs. Dartling,
how would you and your niece like to take charge of
the salads?—under Miss Cane's directions."

The niece hardly had taken her eyes off Captain
Danglers all noon, but turned quickly to the speaker
now.

"Aunty and I will be glad to assume responsibility for the salads, Mrs. Piper," she spoke for the
two.

"And what will I do, Mrs. Piper?" Mrs. Blakeley
inquired.

"Oh, yes, I was just coming to you, Mrs. Blakeley.
I think you will be the proper one to intrust the des-
serts to."

"Oh, but not actually bake!" came aghast.

"Thunderation—*no!*" boomed the Captain again. "Haven't Matey Piper and I just explained that the actual cooking and baking is to be our job? Let you delightful ladies cook and bake? Not a bit of it, eh, Matey?"

"Absolutely not, Skipper," backed up Mr. Clarabel vigorously.

"How unexpressively gallant!" purred Mrs. Clarabel, with a sly look at her husband that made me think she either was laughing at him inside or was getting ready to secretly throttle him. She got a funny look back from him, too—a sort of sheepish look. It was all a puzzle to me then, but wasn't to be a puzzle for very long. Gosh!

"Yes, ladies," the Captain boomed on, "there will be no cooking or baking here for you. Just a few suggestions from you and a little light help along the line that Mrs. Piper has suggested, such as—ah —stirring up the salads—that's all we'll expect from you."

"With Myrtle here to serve, as before," Mrs. Clarabel again took the floor, "I'm sure we're going to get along splendidly. There's just one thing I must insist on, however. Skipper Danglers and Matey Piper, are you listening? I *must* have my gravy."

"Galloping windmills and screeching bobcats!" the Captain almost boomed his head off. "Need I remind you, lady, that you're looking directly at the best gravy maker that ever chased rats out of a ship's galley? If gold medals had ever been awarded for distinguished service at the gravy skillet, I'd be a walking mint—and I'll lay to that!"

"I can make pretty good gravy myself," Mr. Clarabel piped in, not wanting the other cook to get all the attention. "And speaking of medals—"

"Which nicely settles the gravy question," his wife briskly cut him off, with another of those peculiar looks at him. "In fact, everything's settled. I'm driving into town this afternoon, so, Miss Cane, right after we adjourn you and I will get together on the evening meal preparations. This is going to be a lot of fun, just as Miss Martow said. I make the motion, too, that every noon we have a little business meeting like this, to make sure that everything is going along smoothly. Do I hear a second?"

"A second it is, Madam," the Captain's gallant boom drowned out everybody else. "And in turn I make the added motion myself that one of us prepare a suitable expression of sympathy for Mrs. Beesaddle."

"I'll second that motion," Mrs. Clarabel kept up the teamwork between them.

Then she looked around.

"Oh, yes, Miss Garton!—I believe I've heard that along with Miss Cane you're a writer of considerable distinction. Would you like to assume the responsibility for the sympathetic expression just mentioned?"

The girl again had been eyeing the Captain, but as before turned a quick smiling face to the speaker.

"I'd love to, Mrs. Piper. I feel I should add though that I'm not nearly as well known in the writing field as our justly famous Miss Cane. I am, in fact, little more than a beginner."

"But, darling!" her beaming aunt spoke up proudly. "You've had plays on the radio. They were delightful, too."

"Aunty—please! You embarrass me. But, friends, you know what a darling Aunty is!—naturally, she would see only merit in my little plays. What time will you be leaving for town, Mrs. Piper?"

"About two-thirty, I should say. Will that give you time enough to write what you have in mind?"

"Oh, yes—yes, indeed! I can do it in just a few minutes. Mrs. Beesaddle won't care for an elaborate expression—a simple sincere one will please her more. And I'm so glad we can all work together this way to help her. But I've been wondering! Should we expect any help from the lady in number eight? What do you think about that, Captain Danglers?"

She was trying to hook him! She was trying to get him to commit himself in some way or other.

But he wasn't so easily hooked!

"Ahem!" he coughed violently. "Ahem! We have all the help we need. I make the motion we adjourn."

The motion having been seconded, they all got up and filed out.

It was getting more mysterious every minute! But what could it all mean?

I had hoped to get an insight into the mystery when I took the Hideaway Woman her lunch. But I might just as well have set it down in the middle of the ocean for all I heard or saw bearing on the mystery.

The solution though was right there in that peculiarly closed cabin—I was dead sure of that. So the thing to do, I told myself, was to keep as sharp an eye as possible on the cabin and its occupant.

CHAPTER XI

THE POODLE PARLOR

WE GOT two calls during our own meal in the kitchen, a two-buzzer from the Cookbook Woman and a four-buzzer from the Hideaway Woman, to come and get her tray.

Red had scooted off on the first call, hopeful of a nice fat tip, so I took the second call myself, finding the tray with its emptied dishes on the same little porch stand where I had left it. But as before the mysterious woman herself was shut inside. On the way out with the loaded tray, one of the playful airedales got between my legs, tripping me up, the tray and its contents going down ker-bang onto the stone walk outside with me on top of it.

My first thought was to jump up and give the dog a good swift kick where he'd feel it the most. Then a smarter idea came to me.

"Oooo!" I groaned, letting on that I was hurt. *"Oooo!"*

But instead of rushing out to help me, as I had figured she would, thus giving me a chance to get a good look at her and possibly the inside of her cabin, too, the woman simply put in another hurried two-buzz call, bringing Peg on the run.

I clung to him limping as he went off with the trayful of broken dishes.

"How did it happen, Jerry?" he asked sympathetically.

"One of the woman's airedales tripped me up in the porch door.   But tell me as soon as we're out of her sight so I can stop limping."

"Huh?" he stopped dead and stared.

"I'm just pretending," I told him.   "I thought as long as I'd taken the tumble anyway that maybe I could fake a lame leg and get inside.   It didn't work though."

For a minute or two Peg looked as though he was going to bang the tray over my head to give me something genuine to groan about.

Then he started laughing.

"Some detective, you are!" he jeered.   "But wait till Myrtleova the Great sees these broken dishes. Oh-oh!   A ten-cent fine, clumsy, for each broken dish around here!   That's the rule."

"I never got a tip either," I growled.

"Oh, yes, you did!" Peg laughed contentedly. "I picked up a nice shiny half dollar with the broken dishes.   But it's mine now, tumble-heels."

Myrtle was elbow deep in the dishpan when we got back.

"Mr. Kelly was just here," she hurriedly told Peg, sloshing around.   "He didn't know that Mrs. Beesaddle had been injured till I told him.   He's been over to the old hotel waiting for her to bring him his dinner as usual."

"Did he go back there to work?" Peg asked quickly.

"No, I told him he better let the old hotel rest for a few days.   There won't be any more construction

work going on around here anyway till Mrs. Beesaddle gets back, so I couldn't see the sense of just pil-
ing up the lumber—and maybe get into trouble over
it."

Peg tossed me a dish towel.

"All right, big and handsome, just forget about
that mirror in front of you and try massaging some
of these pretty little china plates. But keep your
ears peeled for buzzes from the next room. I'm
going to settle up with Mrs. Switzer now."

"Did you ever hate anybody, Jerry?" Myrtle
asked me long-faced, as we worked together.

"I've seen people I disliked," I admitted, "but I
don't think I ever actually hated anybody. Dad always told me it was wrong to hate people."

"But suppose you had to work for somebody who
hated you?" I was asked further. "Suppose you
were slapped, and told that you were a fool?"

"You don't mean Mrs. Beesaddle?" I asked her,
shocked.

"Jerry," she stopped and looked at me with big
solemn eyes, "Mrs. Beesaddle is the nearest thing to
a mother I've ever known. I'd work my fingers to
shreds for her. But that other woman—that cook
—she was the meanest, the hatefulest, yes and the
trickiest woman I've ever known—and I've known
some pretty mean ones. So you can imagine how
glad I am that she is leaving today. It was her
fault that I had to let some of the cabin work go
this morning, for as soon as news of the accident
came she ordered me to stay in the kitchen. And
now I'm going to tell you something else," the girl
lowered her voice excitedly.

"Yes?" I inquired, wondering what was coming.

"You always smile when I mention my Fairy Caterpillar. But I *do* have a Fairy Caterpillar. When I'm in trouble she helps me.   So this morning she whispered to me: 'Burn the gravy!—and Mrs. Switzer will get mad and quit.'   So I *did* burn the gravy—I not only didn't stir it, as she directed, but I deliberately turned up the fire to make it hotter. Then I danced around till the gravy was all black."

"You're a funny girl, Myrtle," I told her, eyeing her curiously.

"Say, Jerry," she got up a little closer, almost purring now, "what are you doing tonight?   I'd love to take a walk with you in the moonlight."

Oh-oh!

"I think I'll have to stay home and soak my corns," I told her, with a long sigh.

"Good heavens!" she went banging back into the pan.   "Do all the boys around here have sore feet?"

"All the cautious ones do," I told her, grinning.

There were more calls throughout the dishwashing and later sweeping and tidying up, the cook leaving with her pay at the time planned and Miss Garton coming in then to phone her newspaper of her changed plans.

Following the call, she went humming about the room looking idly at the books in the old-fashioned bookcase and at the wall pictures, coming finally to the registration desk.   What she saw in the guest book there evidently greatly pleased her, for she was working her hummer louder than ever when she left.   When I looked at the register though all I could see in it was a bunch of guests' names and cabin numbers.

Myrtle came in from the cabins with an armful of crumpled sheets.

"Well, number seven's all ready for the poodle woman," she told Peg.

"And now for that big dance, huh?" he grinned invitingly.

"I'm too tired to dance now," she sank wearily into a chair.

"Well, listen, Myrtle!" he spoke solicitously. "You've been on the go ever since five o'clock this morning. Why don't you go outside on the lawn with a pillow and rest up?"

"But it'll soon be time to start supper," she looked at the clock.

"Yes, but that isn't your job any longer," he told her quickly. "That's the Captain's and Mr. Clarabel's job now. And, boy, was I tickled this noon when the Captain jumped in that way! He sure is a grand guy, all right—and probably a grand cook, too. You know—I felt pretty shaky when I first started talking. I said we'd soon have a new cook, but I was afraid the change would scare some of the guests out right then. But instead, the first thing I knew everybody was saying, let's do it ourselves— I'll do this and you do that. Now our meal worries are over. And the best part is that there won't be any cook to pay. We'll almost save enough there to pay Mrs. Beesaddle's hospital bill. Boy, will she be pleased when she hears about this!"

"I think myself she'd rather have a paid cook in charge," Myrtle gravely gave her own opinion.

"Huh?" Peg stared. "Say, don't be crazy! Why should she want to pay out good money to a cook when she can get her cooking done free?"

"Yes, but it's easier to tell hired help what to do. You'll almost have to let these men do as they please, as long as they're working for nothing. A regular cook would be out there now getting things started. Besides, how about washday? The cook always helped with the weekly washing. But these men won't help."

"Oh, we can always get some woman to help with the washing. You just leave that to me. But do as I say now—go on outside on the lawn and rest up. Boy, you need a rest."

"How about me?" yawned Red, next-up. "Can I go outside for a rest, too?"

There was a double buzz.

"Sure thing," laughed Peg. "You can go over to number six and read yourself to sleep along with Whoopee."

"What?" squealed Red, when he saw that it was the number six light on. "Do I have to read to that lazy little soup-hound again?"

"Well, don't stand there gloating over it," laughed Peg. "Go on over and see what Mrs. Blakeley wants. I bet a cookie though it is Whoopee."

"Oh, Grandma, what big tonsils you've got," I mimicked Red, as he stamped off.

Then Peg came in.

"Those aren't tonsils, my little granddaughter," he mimicked in pattern. "Those are a couple of English walnuts that I'm saving for dessert."

"Oh, go chew on an old rubber rat," Red fired back at us, "and see if you can't choke to death."

"Tee-hee-hee!" I laughed.

"Ho-ho-ho!" Peg laughed.

Red was back in a few minutes, laughing himself now, with Whoopee in his basket.

"Help yourself, Jerry," the basket was maliciously flopped down beside me on the bench. "Here's a nice little storybook for you to read to him, too, about grandma and her tonsils. So get busy—Mrs. Blakeley's orders."

"What's the big idea?" Peg put in, staring from Red to the dog. "What did you bring him over here for?"

"The big idea is," Red stepped around with vixenish satisfaction, "that Mrs. Blakeley doesn't like my inflection—or whatever she calls it. It's liable to upset Whoopee's nervous system. She's getting ready to drive into town with some of the other ladies, and so she told me to bring Whoopee over here to be read to."

"But why wish him onto me?" I tried to duck the job.

"Because, funny-puss," Red's eyes danced, "you're next-up. Huh! You don't seem to see anything funny about that, do you? It was too funny for anything when you thought I had to go and read to him again—tee-hee-hee!—but it isn't a bit funny when he lands back in your own lap. Well, I think it's awfully funny. HAW-HAW-HAW!"

Whoopee jumped yelping clear out of the basket.

"For Pete's sake!" squawked Peg. "Why don't

you scare the poor dog out of his wits—-with your
crazy bazoo!"

Mrs. Blakeley poked her head in then for a last
look at her pet.

"Toodle-oo!" she waved.

"Bow-wow-wow-wow!" Whoopee replied.

"Mamma's 'ittle precious!" she glowed with
pride.

"Oh, Mrs. Blakeley! Mrs. Blakeley!" Mrs.
Clarabel called from the waiting car.

"Coming, dear!"

"But I want to talk with the Shaw boy. Will you
send him out, please?"

Peg came back puzzling over a slip of paper.

"Take a look at that," he blankly handed the slip
to Myrtle.

"Julienne soup, creamed salsify patties, mushrooms à la casserole, mashed potatoes, green string
beans, orange fritters, marshmallow pudding and
coffee," she read in one long sentence. Then she
turned wonderingly to Peg. "What does it mean?
And where did you get it?"

"Mrs. Clarabel just gave it to me. I'm to give
it to her husband and the Captain when they come in
to get supper. It's what the women have planned
for their first meal."

Red was hanging around me maliciously.

"Well, let's hear a little of Little Red Riding
Hood," he urged. "Don't be a slacker."

But when I started, in a sing-song voice, Peg
stopped me.

"You don't have to read to him when she's gone

—you big sap! Shove him over there in the corner and let him go to sleep himself."

A truck coming noisily in then drew Red to the door.

"It's Horse Foot," he told us, darting out.

"Horse Foot?" Peg's eyes jumped to mine. "Were you still expecting him, Jerry? I thought myself that he'd gone back home."

"That's what I thought, too—he was so long getting here."

"Hey, fellows!" Red yelled to us excitedly. "Come on out—quick! He's brought a kid's playhouse with him."

"Brought what?" I asked, tumbling out, Whoopee for the time being left to shift for himself.

"A kid's playhouse. See?"

That's exactly what it was, too—a complete little two-roomed playhouse, about the size of two piano boxes put together, with a fancy little porch on it, a little bay window, a fake red chimney and everything.

"Wa-al, where do you want it, boys?" the driver asked, as we gathered wonderingly around.

"Yes, where are we g-g-going to put it?" Horse Foot ran around, looking for a good location for it.

"But whatever possessed you to bring it here?" I asked him. "There aren't any kids here but us, and we certainly don't need a playhouse."

"It's our p-p-poodle parlor, Jerry," he explained glowingly. "Y-y-you and Red were talking about one, and now we've got one. Isn't it a h-h-honey?"

A poodle parlor! It would make a good one all right, and a showy one, too—but I certainly never

had expected him to turn up with a thing like this.
Still, I shouldn't have been so greatly surprised
either, for that's the way he was.   You never lacked
for surprises around that egg!

"But where in the world did you get it?" I asked
him, more interested in it now.

"I b-b-borrowed it," he further beamed.

"Borrowed it?—where?"

"Over there w-w-where I got lost," he pointed
vaguely.

"What's he talking about?" Peg dazedly asked
the grinning driver.   "Do you know, mister?"

"Search me," the driver scratched his shaggy
head.   "I think myself he's two-thirds loony.   I
got my pay out of it though, fur totin' it here, so tell
me where you want it and I'll slide it off.   It's just
made of light stuff."

"H-h-here's a good place," Horse Foot called
from near the fountain.

"O.K.," the driver clattered the gears to back up.

"Hey!—stop!" Peg yelled to him.   "You can't
drive across the lawn.   Gee-whillikers!   Look at
the ruts you're making."

"Wa-al, then, where in Sam Hill *do* you want
it?" the driver stopped, scowling.

"We don't want it at all," Peg told him bluntly.

"Listen, smart boy!" the driver leaned down with
an ugly leer.   "I've got my pay fur bringin' it here,
and here it's goin' to stay.   It's either goin' down
over there where young satchel-head says, or right
down here in the middle of your drive.   So make up
your mind."

"Well, just a minute," Peg spoke dazedly.   Then

he ran over to Horse Foot. "Listen, nitwit!—I want to know where you got that thing and what's liable to happen to us if we keep it here. Where did it come from anyway?"

"O-o-over that way," Horse Foot again flourished, "where I g-g-got lost."

Peg's mouth squared.

"Oh!" he scowled. "So you got lost over that way, did you? And seeing some kid's playhouse sitting around unchaperoned you hired this gorilla —I mean this trucker to bring it here. Is that it?"

"S-s-sure thing," Horse Foot beamed. "It'll make a swell poodle parlor. That room w-w-will be the parlor," he pointed, "and that room will be my office."

Peg turned to me dizzily.

"You live the closest to him, Jerry!—suppose you take him for a few minutes while I catch my breath. But don't do anything worse than strangle him."

Horse Foot was laughing now.

"Oh, it's a-a-all right, Jerry," he told me happily. "It's my cousin's playhouse. S-s-she said I could borrow it."

I finally got it out of him that he had taken a wrong turn, after I got out of his sight, finding himself though, after considerable pedaling, in a somewhat familiar rural neighborhood. A very familiar farmhouse came into sight ahead. Where had he seen that house before? Oh, yes—it was Uncle John's house. Or *was* it Uncle John's house? Maybe it was Uncle Ben's house. Yes, it *was* Uncle Ben's house. For Uncle Ben was bald and this house had two chimneys. So Uncle Ben had company for dinner, hearing all about the wonderful new poodle-tending job and the need of a poodle parlor.   There was a Cousin Ella, too, who accommodatingly   owned   a   playhouse.   The   flagged trucker then got into the story, and away went Cousin Ella's playhouse on the truck (Uncle Ben paying the bill!), and now here it was, all ready to be converted into a poodle parlor, with the trucker still fuming because we couldn't decide right off where to put it.

Horse Foot still wanted it by the fountain, so that the coming poodles could look out at the goldfish. And why not?—we finally decided.   So it was put down at the edge of the lawn and carried over, the husky trucker at one end and the four of us wheezing at the other, Myrtle, who had just come out with a pillow, staring open-mouthed.

"That's w-w-what I think, too," said Horse Foot, when the trucker had gone and we were all milling in and out of the pretty little house admiringly, our heads just missing the ceiling.

"You think what?" Peg inquired.

"That I w-w-was pretty smart to find it," Horse Foot beamed.

Peg gave him a slap on the back that almost knocked him down.

"Horse Foot, I used to think that you were petrified from the neck up, but now I'm satisfied you're just petrified from the ears in.   Yes, sir, this is going to make a swell poodle parlor.   But you better get a mop from Myrtle and clean it up a little bit. I'm afraid Cousin Ella wasn't a very neat housekeeper.   And scrape that chewing gum of hers off the door casing. We'll want the house to look its best when the poodle woman arrives. Service, huh? Boy, we'll give her service! A special poodle parlor and a special attendant for her poodles. Could anybody beat that for service? Not in a pig's eye, they couldn't."

CHAPTER XII

IN THE CEMETERY

Mrs. Blakeley rushed in for Whoopee the minute she got home.

"Did mamma's 'ittle precious have a nice restful 'ittle nap?" she cuddled him close to her face.

"Bow-wow-wow-wow!" he spiritedly replied, with an expert lick at her big nose.

I was shivering in my shoes for fear she'd start asking how long he had to be read to before he dropped off, or something like that. But luckily for me she didn't, and picking up the basket I followed her out and down the winding walk to her cabin. There I got the usual fifty-cent tip, stopping on the way back to help Mrs. Clarabel untie an old three-legged rocking chair from the back of her car.

"Where is Mr. Piper?" she inquired crisply, when we got the chair off and down safely on the walk.

"He's over in the kitchen with Captain Danglers studying that supper slip you left for them," I told her.

A dry malicious smile crossed her face.

"Humph! I don't know why they have to study it—such expert cooks as they are! But take that side of the rocker now and help me in the cabin with it. Go easy though and don't scratch it. It's

115

going to finish beautifully when I get another leg on it. All it cost me was ten dollars, too."

Ten dollars for that old thing! It wasn't a starter though to some of the other junk that I found inside. Old three-legged tables, a grandfather's clock without a face or hands, things with shelves to go on the wall and sit in corners, and I can't remember what all. When we finally got the rocker wedged in, there was hardly room to turn around in there.

Peg came running for the supper supplies in the back seat.

"There's something wrong over there, Jerry," he told me soberly, as I helped him get the supplies out.

"Something wrong where?" I asked him.

"Over in the kitchen. But if you're through here, come on and help me carry some of these things over."

"Is there anything else I can do to help you, Mrs. Piper?" I inquired politely, before leaving.

"No, that's all, Jerry. Thanks a heap. Here's a dime for you."

Grabbing the remainder of the supplies, I ran after Peg to the farmhouse where Captain Danglers and Mr. Clarabel were still stupidly scratching their heads over the supper slip.

"Thunderation!" weakly boomed the Captain, plainly stumped. "There's only three things on the whole list that I ever even hears about——the mashed potatoes, the green beans and the coffee. But, Matey, I can make coffee——and I'll lay to that."

"What's the matter?" I asked Peg, as he and

Myrtle stood around with faces a foot long.
"What are they arguing about?"

"They aren't arguing, Jerry," Peg told me soberly. "They've just discovered that neither of
them can cook. And are *we* in a mess now! Oh,
gosh!"

"But they said—" I began, staring at him.

"Sure thing," he cut in, "they said they could
cook, but they can't—the big four-flushers!"

"Oh, dear!" Myrtle groaned in, wringing her
hands. "I was afraid something like this would
happen. We should have hired a regular cook."

"Do you know of anybody around here that we
can get?" Peg asked, with a do-or-die look.

"We might be able to get Mr. Kelly's wife."

"But can she cook?" Peg scowled. "The people
here are paying a big price for their board and
wouldn't be satisfied with just beefsteak and gravy."

"It seems to me," Myrtle thought back quickly,
"that I heard Mrs. Kelly say one time when she was
here that she used to cook at the Woodlawn Bay
hotel. I can phone her and make sure."

"Sure," waggled Peg, "go ahead and call her up.
If she can cook, promise her anything to get her
here. Boy, we can't let those two donkeys spoil
everything now for Mrs. Beesaddle, and break up
her camp! And I was feeling so happy over their
offer! Oh-oh!" he clawed at his hair. "The next
time I'm in town I'm going to have my head examined."

"Do you think the women know that the men are
bluffing?" I asked Peg, as Myrtle flew off to the
phone.

"Mrs. Clarabel certainly knows that her husband is. All she went into the scheme for, with her helpful talk, was to finally show him up and get him back under her thumb again. Don't you remember how she acted, Jerry?—how she looked at him and how he looked back at her? He knew then that she was after him. He thought, though, that Captain Danglers could save him. That big supper list was just a test of Mrs. Clarabel's to see what the Captain himself could do—for she got herself on the planning committee, you remember! I don't know how much the other women really know, but clever little Mrs. Clarabel is just leading them along to gain her own ends. But listen to the men now!—what they're saying about it."

"If you'd just given me a hint, Matey," Captain Danglers stamped around wild-eyed.

"But, Skipper, you're the one who suggested it in the first place. I thought—"

"Yes, I know! I know!" the Captain stopped, with a wild flourish of his arms. "But I was depending on you. Thunder and blazes! I always was a tarnation old fool when it came to pleasing the ladies—the dear, sweet, adorable ladies! It's just my nature to promise 'em anything they ask for. If one of them was to say, 'Oh, Captain, please get me the moon!'—it's a fact, Matey, I'd risk my old fool neck trying to comply. Yes, sir, that's the kind of a soft-hearted old gilly I am." He started pacing again, his peg leg going thump, thump, thump! "But wouldn't this put a wrinkle in your anchor though? The two of us promising to do the cooking and each depending on the other."

"Well, I told you why I did it," gloomed Mr. Clarabel. "I just got to the point today where I wasn't going to let my wife boss me any more. So when she said I *couldn't* cook—right there in front of everybody that way—well, right then I got up on my ear and said I *could* cook."

"Thinking that I could, eh?"

"Exactly, Skipper. Exactly."

"Humph!" the Captain glowered at the slip. "Mushrooms à la casserole. That must mean mushrooms *in* a casserole—and a casserole is a baking dish. I know that much."

Mr. Clarabel, too, took another look at the list.

"And that Julienne soup—maybe that has something to do with the Romeo and Juliet play that the actress was talking of putting on here," he made the wild guess.

"Say, Matey!" a crafty light came into the Captain's eyes. "I've got an idea! Let's let on that the cook stole the casserole, and cross the mushrooms off. What say you to that? We can say she took the soup kettle, too."

Myrtle came flying back, new hope in her eyes.

"She's coming, Peg! Her husband's bringing her over in their car. I promised her twenty dollars a week. She'll be here in less than ten minutes, she said."

I don't know what the supper would have been like that night if the neighbor woman hadn't come, for most certainly those two men never could have cooked a satisfactory supper, or saved their face with their intended trickery either. Mrs. Kelly's supper though was perfect. You should have seen the surprise on the guests' faces—Mrs. Clarabel's particularly—as first the Romeo and Juliet soup was brought in, then the mushrooms à la casserole and everything else as ordered, clear down to the marshmallow pudding and coffee. Supper was a little bit late, with the country darkness creeping in outside, but when the food finally came it brought only the warmest praise.

"Well, mamma," Mr. Clarabel went in importantly in his big kitchen apron to inquire, "has everything been satisfactory?"

"Yes," his wife complimented, "it's one of the finest meals I ever ate. But how much of it did *you* cook?"

"Well, now," he drawled, with hidden eyes, "that would be hard to say. You see, the Captain and I have discovered that we have practically the same technique, so we're working together on everything."

Yes—the two big four-flushers!—they were working together all right, having offered Mrs. Kelly an extra ten dollars a week to help them keep up the deception, arguing that it was just a little joke among the guests after all, and nothing for her to hesitate about. The idea was for her to slip in and cook each meal as ordered by the planning committee, then slip out and let the two big shots dish it up.

"Well, it's them for it," Peg himself wearily washed his hands of the whole affair. "If we tried to interfere, the men probably would leave here anyway, and maybe when the women get wise they'll all leave. But I'm not going to worry about it.

No one can say that I haven't done the best I could here today. And has it been a day! Oh, boy! Oh, boy! It seems as though I've lived a whole summer since I first got up this morning. But there goes the buzzer. You better take the call, Jerry, while the rest of us help Myrtle with the dishes. It looks like Mrs. Clarabel's light from here. If it is her, ask her if she saw anything of Mr. Beesaddle at the hospital this afternoon. He should have been home to milk the cows hours ago."

"Oh, didn't I tell you?" Myrtle spoke up from the dishpan. "He phoned before supper that he's staying overnight at the hospital. I got Mr. Kelly to do the milking. He's going to milk tomorrow morning, too, when he brings his wife over to get breakfast."

Having strung an electric light wire from the farmhouse to the poodle parlor, Horse Foot was sitting out there now, in his white coat, awaiting the arrival of the famous apricot poodles. His light gave the dancing fountain a peculiar eerie look. I had the crazy feeling, too, as I ran down the winding walk, that queer-shaped squirming things were lurking in the deepening shadows. Night in the country has always seemed deeper and quieter to me than night in town. And that last closed cabin lent an air of mystery to the place that certainly didn't help a fellow's nerves any.

Mrs. Clarabel and her three nearest neighbors, all beautifully dressed, were cramped into one corner of the jammed cabin playing bridge when I got there, Mr. Clarabel himself having driven alone into town for an evening newspaper.

"Would it be possible, Jerry, for us to get some coffee and sandwiches a little later on?" I was asked, when the cards were gathered up for another deal.

"I think so," I nodded. "What kind of sandwiches would you like?"

"Let's not have anything heavy," hastily put in the actress. "Dear me! We soon won't be able to get into our clothes if we have many meals like the one tonight. Just the coffee alone would satisfy me."

"Yes, let's just have the coffee," Mrs. Dartling took the same view.

"Very well," Mrs. Clarabel told me, anxious to get back to her cards. "A pot of coffee at ten, and some ice water now. Oh, yes, bring some milk, too, for Merry and Diggs—they've been acting hungry. What did you bid in, Miss Garton?—did you say clubs?"

Myrtle and Red were working alone on the dishes when I got back.

"Do *you* have sore feet, too?" she asked him, over the dishpan.

"Sore feet?" he stared at her. "What do you mean?"

"Last night I hinted to Peg that I'd like to go walking with him in the moonlight, but he said he couldn't—he had sore feet. Tonight Jerry gave me the same excuse, when I hinted to him." She edged closer. "I was just wondering if—"

Red began dancing crazily on one foot.

"Oh, boy!" he howled. "Do my dogs ever hurt me tonight!"

"Huh!" Myrtle banged back into the dishpan. "I think I'll go to bed when the dishes are done."

One of us, at least, was supposed to stay on duty till the guests were all in bed, after which, for emergency purposes, the buzzer-board was connected with a special loud buzzer in the dormitory. But with Myrtle waiting up to make the ordered coffee, there was no special need of the three of us hanging around there, too. We had a nice little scheme in our mind now and promising to double whatever she got in tips if she'd service the calls for an hour or two, we got some soiled sheets from a hamper in the basement and a bag of cobs, and started out in the direction of the Woodlawn Bay hotel.

As Peg had said, if the Strickers came at all, as they so cockily had threatened to do, the chances were ten to one that they'd come down the road, as the wooded jungle around the old Windmere house was no place to force through at night. So why not get ahead of the enemy, to the little private cemetery that we had noticed almost directly opposite the Windmere entrance and wait for them there, first scaring the wits out of them with our sheets and then triumphantly running them back to the hotel with a lively cob barrage?

Horse Foot couldn't very well go along on account of the poodles, which were due to arrive any minute now, so rather than start an argument with him we just slipped out without him. Keeping to the side of the moonlit road, with a sharp watch ahead, we came presently to the Windmere thicket on the right and then the little neglected cemetery

on the left, with its leaning tombstones and surrounding unkempt hedge.

A cemetery is no more dangerous than any other
similar reserved spot, either by day or night, but
frankly I've never seen one yet that I wouldn't
dodge at night if possible. So as you can very well
imagine I didn't let husky old Peg get very far away
from me.

"Now, listen," he told us in a low voice, as we lay
waiting behind the hedge. "When the Strickers get
here, don't jump up too quick—and for Pete's sake
don't either of you laugh. I'll give the signal when
they're directly opposite—then come up slowly over
the hedge, like a ghost actually coming out of a
grave, and let out a gurgling drawn-out moan, like
this: O-o-o-o-o-o! Do you get the idea?"

"You sounded more like a sick cow to me," tittered Red.

"Listen, feller!" came stiffly. "That's just as
good a moan as any real ghost could give. Just see
that you do as well when the time comes. I'm hoping the Strickers will notice the cemetery ahead, for
that will get them in the right mood for a good
scare. Or if they don't happen to notice it, we'll
just come up anyway like I told you. The minute
they hear us they'll stop dead in their tracks. Boy,
can't you see the look on their faces? I sure can.
They'll be expecting to find us at the farm—they'll
never dream of a trick like this. They'll think it's
three real ghosts—and, boy, will they ever leg it for
shelter!"

"Yes," giggled Red, "I can imagine how they'll
travel, especially Jum Prater with those big feet of

his. I'm just wondering if we'll be able to keep within range of them with our cobs."

"I wish they'd hurry and come," I shivered.

Peg looked at me curiously.

"What's the matter with you, Jerry? Surely you aren't cold! I thought it was a swell summer's night myself."

"It's that crazy cemetery," I explained, with an uneasy look around. "I have the feeling all the time that something's going to come out of one of those old graves and scare *us*."

Presently from somewhere in back of the cemetery a dog barked. Then a slow-moving black figure came into sight through the tombstones and bushes, entering the cemetery at the back and coming almost directly toward us.

Gosh! If you must know the actual truth, I never was so scared in all my life. Not that I thought for one instant that it was a ghost—I saw right off that it was a woman in a black dress. I knew, from the two dogs with her, what woman it was, too. But right then, after what I had heard about her and what I had been thinking about her myself, she seemed to me a hundred times more dangerous than any ghost.

It was the Hideaway Woman out with her dogs on one of her peculiar night tramps!

CHAPTER XIII

A STRANGE FLIGHT

PEG went into the hedge on all fours, hissing to us to follow him with our sheets, the Hideaway Woman and her two scampering dogs getting closer to us every second.

I suppose it was silly of me to be so scared of her, for if caught the worst that could possibly happen to us would be a sharp scolding. We weren't doing anything unlawful, and certainly we had just as much right there as she had herself. In a way, we had more right, for she was snooping around with hidden things behind her that *could* be unlawful, while we were just out to have some natural boyish fun. But just the same I wanted to escape her if I could, and lost no time following Peg into the hedge as directed.

Red was having trouble with his sheet.

"Gol-ding!" he muttered under his breath, giving the sheet a yank.

"What's the matter?" Peg breathed.

"My sheet's stuck on a bush."

Our biggest danger was from the dogs. They'd almost certainly smell us, and either force us to come out or skin out. But that sheet of Red's saved the day for us!

There was a loud rip as he further pulled at it. Gosh, it sounded like a thunderclap to me! The woman, of course, stopped dead—the two bristling dogs with her. Then as she saw something white tear loose from a bush and disappear in a flash into the hedge, like a ghost's shirttail, she let out a frightened scream, running into the road and off in the direction of the pet farm as fast as she could go, her dogs after her.

"Oh, boy! Was that ever a narrow escape for us!" I gurgled weakly, dropping flat on the ground.

"Yes," Peg looked gravely after the flying figure, "but I'm sorry we scared her. I wouldn't have done that purposely for anything. Shall we follow her and apologize, fellows?"

"And get a bawling out?" piped Red. "Huh! What would be the sense in that—as long as she didn't see us?"

"Yes, but she may shiver all night, thinking it was a ghost she saw," Peg further worried about it.

"Any woman who hasn't better sense than to go prowling around a place like this at night ought to shiver," declared Red. "You couldn't get my mother to do that for a thousand dollars."

"This woman is a whole lot older than your mother, Red."

"Which is all the more reason why she should stay at home nights and knit," Red said flatly.

"There's something blamed queer about her, all right," I put in.

"Yes," studied Peg, "I'm wondering myself if she wasn't hanging around here for a reason. Certainly, if she just wanted to exercise her dogs she wouldn't pick out a cemetery to do it in."

"She came from in back," I uneasily looked back through the tombstones.

"Yes," Peg gasped quickly, "and there's someone else coming from in back, too! Down, fellows! Quick!"

"Suffering cats!" squawked Red. "What's going on back there anyway?—are the ghosts having a jamboree?"

"Pipe down—*you!*" Peg hissed.

This time it was a man we saw!—he came running, as though weirdly frightened about something.

"Why! It's Captain Danglers!" gasped Peg, as the panting runner came out into a particularly bright patch of moonlight and took to the road.

"And he had a revolver in his hand!" Red gasped in turn. "He's chasing the woman down the road. He's going to shoot her!"

We took off then ourselves, keeping the peg-legged runner in sight all the way to the farm. But there were no shots ahead as we expected. The last cabin, when we got there, was dark and silent, and the Captain himself, in his own cabin, was lazily stretching before quietly retiring.

"Someone give me a pinch," said Peg in a daze. "I want to find out if I'm dreaming."

"With pleasure," giggled Red. "There!—take that."

"Ouch!" cried Peg. "You don't have to pinch a chunk out, you ape! I guess I'm awake all right. But if that isn't the dumfoundest thing *I* ever heard of. What do you make of it, Jerry? You've got the idea that you're a pretty good detective. Tell

us what the two were doing in the cemetery and why
he chased her home with a gun."

"But *did* he chase her home with a gun?" I
thought hard on the riddle.

"What are you trying to argue?—that it was a
cucumber pickle that he had in his hand?" snorted
Peg. "Of course it was a gun. Wasn't it, Red?"

"It sure looked like a gun to me," Red agreed.

"Yes, but maybe he wasn't chasing her to *harm*
her, as we thought," I tugged harder at the riddle.
"Maybe he was running after her to *protect* her."

"Say!" Peg then did some quick thinking of his
own. "That's an idea! Come to think of it now
—when she started out last night with her dogs (I
heard them and saw her) he *did* take in after her.
That's what he was doing again tonight. He was
secretly following her around to protect her from
something. No wonder he came tearing popeyed
through the cemetery when he heard that scream!
But what did he suspect had happened to her?
What is there around here that he's protecting her
from? Gee-miny crickets, guys! I'm getting
goose pimples! Do you suppose there's something
prowling around here nights that's liable to lay us
out if we get in its way?"

Red's teeth started playing a tune.

"L-l-let's get in where it's light," he chattered.

Horse Foot was sitting all alone in the office
when we went in, looking like the last rose of summer.

"S-s-she's crazy," he scowled.

"Who?" asked Peg.

"That P-p-poodle Woman. Just because I let one

of her poodles fall in the f-f-fountain, she said, 'Are you deaf, too?' I said, 'No, m-m-ma'am.' Then she said, 'Well, you're dumb enough to be.' Then she y-y-yanked all her poodles out of the poodle parlor and took them to b-b-bed with her in her cabin."

"When did she get here?" Peg asked quickly.

"About an hour ago. But w-w-where have you fellows been?"

"Oh, out fooling around. But, listen, clumsy!— the woman didn't say anything about leaving tomorrow morning, did she?—because of what you did?"

"No. S-s-she likes it here. She don't like me though."

"Huh!" put in Red, with his nose up. "Who could?"

"My m-m-ma does," Horse Foot spunked up.

"Did Myrtle show the woman to her cabin?" Peg next asked.

"No, I d-d-did."

"But where was Myrtle?"

"I'm in here, Peg," the girl spoke quietly for herself from an adjoining darkened room. "Turn out the light—I want to tell you something. I've been waiting for you."

"Turn out the light?—what do you mean? Are your eyes hurting you?"

"I want to make sure that I'm not seen through the window."

"Oh, you're kidding!" Peg snorted. "Come on out and quit acting so silly."

"Not till you turn out the light."

"Oh, all right then. Red—you're by the switch

—give it a twist. There! Is that dark enough for you, mysterious?"

"I'm going to leave," the girl then spoke closer.

"Say, what's the matter with you tonight?" Peg asked earnestly. "Are you crazy?"

There was a low sob.

"Oh, gee, Myrtle!" Peg's voice softened. "What's the matter anyway? Gosh, if it's something we've done—"

"No, it isn't that," the girl spoke between sobs. "You boys have been just grand to me. So has Mrs. Beesaddle. That's why I'm crying—because I—I have to leave."

"Boy, this sure has been a night of riddles," Peg spoke in a daze. "You say you're going to leave and then you say you're crying about it. That makes about as much sense to me as a blind man's spectacles. Can't you make it a little plainer? I suppose we could get along without you, if we had to, but you're going to leave an awful hole here, I can tell you that much. Is it just because you're tired, Myrtle? Gee, I hope so. Why don't you go to bed now, and maybe you'll be all right by morning. You can sleep a little later than usual, too. We'll get everything going, won't we, fellows?"

"And, how!" Red and I spoke together.

"Yes," the girl spoke less emotionally now, "you boys will have to start things tomorrow morning, as I won't be here myself. I'm leaving tonight. I'm leaving in the dark, too, the same as I'm now talking to you in the dark. I can't tell you where I'm going, and you mustn't try to follow me. I'm afraid that

—that something terrible is going to happen here. I want to prevent it if I can. Good-by!"

"Oh, but, Myrtle!—hey, wait!" Peg cried frantically. "Where are you? Red! Turn on the light—gosh! I believe she's gone!"

She was, too! When the light came on, with us all staring white-faced at each other, there was no sign of her.

"Did I hear someone say something around here about having a lot of *fun?*" Red gurgled. "Boy, I don't call *this* fun! If you want to know the plain truth, I feel about as funny as a man would who was getting ready to have his head sliced off in one of those French gilly-machines. Eek!—like that!" he gruesomely sliced at his throat with his flattened hand.

Peg came back scowling from the back door.

"Did she tell *you* anything?" he bluntly asked Horse Foot.

"N-n-no."

"But something must have happened here tonight to scare her off—and you were here all evening. Haven't you any idea at all what it is? Try using your brain a little bit now. It's a strain on you, I know—but try anyway."

"Try w-w-what?" Horse Foot inquired sleepily.

"Oh, gosh!" Peg turned away disgusted. "Let's grab a lunch, fellows, and roll in. I'm tired of working on riddles myself. If something's going to happen, let it happen, and we'll make the best of it. It isn't our farm—and I'm not going to worry myself daffy over it. I'm not going to waste any more sleep waiting for those Strickers either. It looks like they've backed out anyway."

It was now well along toward eleven. The cabins were all in darkness. Sleepy ourselves, we locked up, after a hasty light lunch, and with all the lights out except the few dim night lights in the cabin row, we set out together down the dormitory path with a flashlight.

Ahead, Peg got the key from its hiding place and unlocked the door.

"Ho-hum!" he yawned, dropping wearily onto his bed. "Will I ever pound my ear tonight! I've been on the go ever since five o'clock this morning."

"Five o'clock?" squealed Red, kicking off his shoes. "We don't all have to get up that early, do we?"

"No," yawned Peg, with a wink at me, "just the four of us. You can sleep till eight yourself. With that face of yours, you need a beauty nap."

Red quickly counted heads.

"Hey, you big gyp!" he squawked. "That's all there is of us is four."

"Well, figure it out," Peg went on undressing.

Having picked out the third bed for himself, Red got in grumbling.

"Five o'clock! That's a swell time for a bell-boy to get up! What do we have to do here?— go around and wake up the chickens?"

"You'll be lucky," laughed Peg, "if you don't get called out in the middle of the night. I did last night. One of the number four cookbook cats started yowling for milk."

"By the way," I asked Peg quickly. "Did you switch the buzzer here all right?"

"Oh, sure! And, boy, if it goes off you'll hear it!—it sounds like a young boiler factory turning handsprings. It's up there on the wall in that box."

"But how do you know which cabin to go to?" I studied the box. "I don't see any lights."

"Use your head, Jerry! If you were in one of the cabins and had to put in an emergency call, wouldn't you turn on your own light?"

"Oh, sure!" I flushed. "I didn't think of that. But who's next-up? Does anybody know?"

"Sure, Horse Foot is," Red said promptly.

"Go lay an egg," I told him. "Horse Foot isn't even a bellboy. I think myself it's you, lame brain."

He peeked through the window near him.

"Well, I'm not going out there alone—not after that cemetery stuff and what Myrtle told us," he rebelled. "If someone does buzz during the night, one of you fellows will have to go with me."

"Oh, I'll go," Peg settled it, anxious to get to sleep. Then he reached for the long light cord near his bed. "But everybody into the sheets now—for out goes the light."

"Boy, this sure is a swell bed," Red squirmed around to make himself a comfortable nest.

"Oh-oh!" grunted Peg. "That's another job for us."

"What?" I asked quickly.

"Making up the cabin beds. We'll sure miss Myrtle all right! And, doggone!—do I ever feel like kicking myself for letting her get away that way. We could have stopped her and made her tell what she knew, if we'd had our wits about us. I've been mad about it ever since."

Afraid that he'd get the bedmaking job, too, Red crazily started snoring. Nor was it long before we joined him, one after another, for you know how boys are when they're tired out.

I was the last one to drop off. I remember lying there wondering what had happened, after we left the farmhouse, to drive Myrtle away so mysteriously, and what further was liable to happen there. Had she taken a long-distance call for the Hideaway Woman or the Captain (who were both out), thus learning of some sinister peril dogging the woman?

No, it couldn't be that. It was something that concerned Myrtle herself. Well, when morning came I'd find out if there had been any phone calls, and pin Horse Foot down sharper, too. I'd further keep a closer eye on that last cabin, for certainly there must be some tie between Myrtle's flight and the known mystery there.

But where had she fled to? What was she planning to do?—for she said she was going to try and prevent "something terrible" from happening, if she could.

I got up at this point and locked the door. But first I took a peek out. The moon was buried in black clouds now. I could just dimly make out the outline of the surrounding trees. Under the trees everything was ink.

The door locked, I got back shivering into bed. There were a few more scattered jumbled thoughts. Then with the others I dropped off.

CHAPTER XIV

POODLE TENDER!

AT TWELVE-THIRTY we were up again with still another mystery on our hands. Horse Foot had slipped out while we were asleep, locking the door behind him. Peg and Red had discovered the locked door and empty bed when they went to go out to answer an emergency call, then wonderingly getting me up.

Determined to get out somehow, Peg ran around to all the windows, hoping to find a loose screen. Failing, he finally knocked one out with the fireplace poker.

I had followed him around from window to window, finding now that everything outside was bright moonlight again. The clouds that had banked out the moon when last I looked out had all disappeared. On the west and north sides I could see clear across to the Windmere woods in one direction and back to the back grove in the other. There was no sign of Horse Foot though in either direction. Nor could I see anything of him in the trees and shrubbery on the two other sides.

The screen knocked out, Peg went out through the small high opening on his stomach, telling us to hang to his feet and let him down easy. That wasn't so easily done however. He took a drop in spite of us, groaning as he landed on his hands and head. He was up again though in just a second or two.

"All right, fellows," he panted through the window. "Come on through like I did and I'll catch you."

"Did you hurt yourself?" I asked him, when we were all together outside.

"Oh, just a bump on the head," he dismissed it indifferently. Then he started off toward the cabins. "Come on! Let's find out who that call is from, for there goes the buzzer again. We'll look for Horse Foot afterwards."

The little gray monkey peculiarly took after us in the cabin drive, following us chattering to the last lighted cabin where the Hideaway Woman was having a bad spell with her heart. She was sitting on the edge of her bed when we got there, in a long white nightgown, her revealed wrinkled face as white now as the nightgown itself. She thought herself that she was dying, and gasping, begged one of us at least to stay with her while the others ran to phone for a doctor.

Peg said he'd stay, so Red and I ran back up the winding drive to the farmhouse, the chattering monkey still after us.

Getting in and to the phone, I asked the night operator to get one of the Tutter doctors on the line just as quickly as possible.

"Have you any preference?" she asked crisply.

"No," I told her quickly. "Anyone will do, just so he gets here quick."

"Then I'll call Doctor Leland," she decided.

"Sure thing," I agreed. "Call Doc Leland.

He's a good doctor. He always doctors me when I'm sick."

I could hear a long ring at the other end, then Doc's wheezing grunty voice came sleepily.

"Yes?"

"Say, Doc," I told him quickly, "this is Jerry Todd. I'm over at Mrs. Beesaddle's cabin colony south of town. There's a woman here with a bad heart. She wants you to come over right away. Will you?"

"Oh, I suppose so," came wearily. "Yes, I'll be there. Goo'-by."

This was a good time, I figured, to learn if there had been any earlier long-distance calls for either the Hideaway Woman or the peg-legged Captain.

"What was the party's name, please?" the operator asked, when I got her on the wire again and started questioning her.

"Mrs. Hannah Topple," I gave the name.

There was a short pause.

"Sorry," the reply then came, "we have no record of any calls between eight and ten for that party."

"Maybe the call was for Captain Otis Danglers," I gave that name.

There was another short pause.

"Sorry, we have no record of any calls during that period for that party."

"Well, was there a call between eight and ten for Myrtle Bean?" I asked finally.

"Sorry, we have no record of any calls during that period for that party, or any other party on your line. Did you wish another number?"

"No, that's all," I told her. "And thanks for
the information."

So there hadn't been any long-distance calls, as I
had suspected. Then, Myrtle must have overheard
something or had seen or been told something, leading up to her mysterious flight. Eliminating the
Hideaway Woman and the Captain, both away at
the time, I quickly checked over the others in camp.
There certainly was no mystery about Mr. and Mrs.
Clarabel or the actress either. Similarly I checked
out the Cookbook Woman and the Pekingese woman
in number six. That left just the new poodle woman
and the young newspaper woman and her aunt in
number three.

The Poodle Woman! Um. There was something to think about. I hadn't given her a thought
before. Mrs. Hetty Hinds the third! It certainly
was an important-sounding name. Almost too important-sounding in fact. Could it be possible, I
asked myself with growing excitement, that there
was something phoney about the new woman? Further, was there something dangerous about her, so
very dangerous, in fact, that Myrtle, knowing her,
had fled from her in deadly fear?

I was still puzzling over the riddle, my thoughts
swinging first one way and then another, when Doc
Leland drove in at one. The stricken woman was
in no particular danger, he told us, as we waited anxiously outside. It was more her nerves than her
heart. She had had some kind of a bad scarce, but
by morning would be all right again. We made two
trips to the farmhouse for him, once for hot water
and once for cold, feeling pretty guilty, for we knew

more about the mentioned scare than he did. The patient was sleeping when he left, about one-thirty.

Again locking up, we trudged wearily down the dormitory path, hoping that we'd find Horse Foot there when we got there. Sure enough, there he sat half asleep on the dormitory steps.

"D-d-did you fellows hear him, too?" he asked us, big-eyed, when we shook him awake.

"Hear who?" grunted Peg.

"The m-m-man on the roof."

"Are you sure it wasn't the man in the moon?" Peg snorted skeptically.

"W-w-what kind of shoes does he wear?" Horse Foot asked promptly.

Of all the crazy questions!

"Go on inside and go back to bed," I told him, completely disgusted with him.

The last I remember he was growling to himself in bed because we wouldn't believe him. There *had* been a man on the roof! He had *heard* the man, so he had!——he guess *he* knew! He could prove it, too, for there were *footprints* behind the dormitory showing where the man had jumped down when he heard the door being unlocked! It was at this point that I floated off beyond the sound of his voice. Then suddenly I awoke choking.

I thought at first that someone actually had me by the throat. I could hardly breathe. The other fellows were all up choking, too.

"Haw-haw-haw-haw!" a familiar jeering voice came through one of the open windows. "What's the matter in there, pussycat tenders? Don't you like our pepper?"

Pepper! Yes, that's what it was! The Strick-ers were out there pumping burning pepper in on us. They had the door tied too. It probably was them that Horse Foot had earlier heard on the roof. Hidden near by, when he went out alone, they could easily have picked him up, but had waited instead till we were all together in bed again. What they had for us they wanted us all to get.

And though it galls me to admit it, I'll have to confess that we got plenty. They had an old bee-smoker. We could hear it go puff, puff, puff at one of the windows. With each puff more peppery smoke came in.

Bid Stricker is a good example of what a boy can be who tries to make himself as tough as his sur-roundings. He calls my gang the "Stuck-uppers," priding himself on the fact that *he* comes from Zulu-town, the town's toughest quarter. He accuses us too, of trying to run the town, simply because for the most part we live on Main street, and has the kids in his own end thinking that they have to keep fight-ing us all the time to protect their own rights. His chief ally is his cousin, Jimmy Stricker. Others in the gang are Chet Milden and mouthy Jum Prater, all working now at the Woodlawn Bay hotel. I've already told you about Red's big mouth, but, oh, boy, what he had in the front of his face was a mere pinhole as compared to what Jum Prater had. Na-ture even had made his ears different so that his mouth could spread farther back. It was him now who was working the blower.

"Shall I put in some more pepper, Bid?" he yelled.

"Sure thing," Bid yelled back from somewhere

overhead. "Give 'em some of the red pepper this time. Let's make 'em do some real coughing."

Peg got us all to the door then, telling us choking and gasping to pull like sixty. If we didn't get out before the red pepper came, he told us, we were goners.

"Here they come, Bid!" screeched Chet Milden on guard, as the door finally flew open, giving us escape.

Getting this signal, Bid and Jimmy overhead dumped two pails of dirty water down on us as we tumbled out. To this day I don't know where they got the water, or what they had in it, but it certainly wasn't perfume, I can tell you that! Oh, oh, what a stinking mess! It was all a complete triumph for Bid and his gang, who got safely away while we were clawing the filthy water out of our eyes, and an equally complete defeat for us. But there were other nights coming, we told each other fiercely, as we stripped and washed ourselves in the moonlit cow tank. The Strickers would pay plenty for this.

The dormitory was still too full of peppery smoke to think of sleeping there, so we got some pillows and finished out the night on the office floor, Mrs. Kelly awakening us when she came at seven to get breakfast.

Again the Captain and Mr. Clarabel took full credit for the finely prepared meal, Mrs. Kelly herself having quietly slipped away as agreed. It was funny, in a way, to watch the two big bluffs as they paraded around the kitchen in their white caps and aprons, though we were too anxious about the final outcome to do much grinning over it. Red and I

BID AND JIMMY DUMPED TWO PAILS OF
DIRTY WATER DOWN ON US.

did the serving that morning, Peg taking over the
first daily pet feeding. With the exception of the
monkey and the birds, the pets were all given two
regular feedings, at eight in the morning and around
four-thirty in the afternoon, the dogs getting dried
wholewheat bread soaked in beef juice and the cats
getting milk and scraps of the chopped-up beef.
Bones were never given to the pets at any time.
There had been a lot of chicken bones left over the
first day I was there—the finest dog feed in the
world, I thought—but, no, sir, every bone had to be
burned, as chicken bones particularly were supposed
to be bad for high-toned dogs' intestines.

"Is Myrtle ill this morning?" Mrs. Clarabel inquired solicitously, when I came around with her
second cup of coffee.

"No, ma'am," I explained. "She left last night."

"Left?" the word was accompanied by a lift of
the speaker's eyebrows. "And Mrs. Beesaddle
gone too? Surely you aren't going to try and run
this place with just men and boys!"

"We're all going to do the best we can—at least
till Mr. Beesaddle himself gets back to take charge,"
I told her.

"Just a minute!" she stopped me, as I started off.
"Please bend down as I want to speak confiden-
tially."

"Yes, ma'am," I complied wonderingly.

"Now, tell me the truth," she spoke in a terse
inquisitive voice. "Did Captain Danglers actually
prepare that wonderful meal last night?"

"He helped," I told her, hoping she wouldn't pin
me down too close.

"Well, he certainly must be a marvel," she declared, with a wondering air. Then she straightened stiffly. "But of course by now you know the truth about my husband. *He* can't boil water himself without burning it."

"He's helping with all the meals," I declared, with a sober face.

"Helping! Poof! And *him* telling the ladies that he always did the cooking at home! I never was so mortified in all my life—for they actually believed it, and still do for that matter—the big windbag! But if he and Captain Danglers can keep things going in the kitchen till Mrs. Beesaddle gets back, I'll never interfere myself. Certainly, the meals so far are beyond criticism."

Peg here laughingly beckoned me into the kitchen.

"Well, Jerry," he told me, "I guess you're it."

"It—what?" I asked bluntly.

"Poodle tender extraordinary to her highness Mrs. Hetty Hinds the third. Boy, is she ever a bejeweled dowager! Um-um! And wait till you see those poodles! They're all a sort of reddish brown —apricot, she calls it—and worth a thousand dollars apiece. It'll be almost a steady job for you brushing and combing them, for around their head and halfway down their body they have hair a foot long. She keeps it tied up with fancy ribbons. The rest of their body is trimmed skin tight, except for a few hairy bunches here and there. Boy, they sure are aristocrats!"

Horse Foot stood listening.

"Is s-s-she still mad at me?" he asked long-faced.

"Listen, clumsy!" Peg waved him off. "You're entirely out of the picture—after what you did to her precious poodle last night. It'll be pots and pans for you if you stay. She wouldn't have a redhead either, she just told me. That left just us two, Jerry."

"Well, how about yourself?" I growled. "I'm not so crazy over the job, let me tell you. I'd rather have something with a little more variety —than to sit all day and brush a flock of poodles."

"Sure," Peg agreed quickly, "I'll take the job if you feel that way about it. I thought though you'd rather do it than make beds."

"There's still Horse Foot and Red to make the beds," I further tried to escape that job too.

"Listen, Jerry, those two kids are going to have plenty to do without making beds and cleaning cabins. I was going to do that myself, being the biggest. But if you'd rather do it—"

"No," I quickly decided, "I think I'll take the poodles in preference to the beds."

"Fine!" Peg's eyes glowed over my decision. "I think myself, Jerry, that you're the best one here for that job. It *is* a very important job, too, I want to tell you. And you won't have to be brushing them all the time either—you can take them out on the lawn and have a lot of fun with them. They look kind of sissified with their ribbons and fancy hair trims, but I bet they're plenty smart. If you ask me, I think you've got the best job of all."

"Yes, but how about the tips?"

"The Poodle Woman tipped swell this morning when I was around feeding, so I think you'll come out all right on that.   Anyway, let's let it stand that way, for a few days at least.   If you find then that you don't like the job I'll try and get her to take Red, or take the job myself."

"And will I have to move into the poodle parlor out in front?" I asked, with a silly laugh.

I never had dreamed I'd wind up there!

"Sure thing," Peg waggled.   "It's your poodle parlor now.   You and Red wanted one, so now you've got one.   It won't be exactly as you planned, but still it'll be pretty much of a beautifying parlor at that, as the whole purpose of the brushing is to make the dogs' coats as shiny and glossy as possible for the coming London show."

"Say, Peg!" I asked eagerly.   "Do you believe that?"

"Believe what?"

"That there really is a London show?—and that the poodle woman is what she pretends to be?"

"Whatever made you think she wasn't?" he stared.

I told him then the things that I had been thinking over.   But he just laughed at me.   Whatever lay back of Myrtle's mysterious flight, he declared, with some fixed views of his own, the Poodle Woman had nothing to do with it.   It was something connected somehow with the Hideaway Woman and Captain Danglers.

CHAPTER XV

THE DEAD POODLE

Mrs. Hinds was a big surprise to me when I met her. From Peg's description of her I had expected to find a robust commanding type of woman well into her fifties—that being my idea of a "bejeweled dowager." What I actually found in number seven though was a slim pretty blond-haired blue-eyed woman of scarcely more than thirty, apparently very clever and certainly very decisive.

Having crisply outlined my duties, she began quizzing me in a light curious way about the camp in general. How many cabins were there? Who occupied them? What kind of pets did the other guests have? Did any of them have poodles? Were any of them professional pet exhibitors?

To all of my answers she gave an attentive ear, seeming peculiarly relieved when I told her, in answer to her final question, that so far as I knew she was the only exhibitor there.

"I had hoped to be entirely relieved of the care of my poodles during my rest here," she told me in conclusion. "That is why I specified a trained attendant in my wire. It seems though that no effort was made to carry out my wishes."

"There are no trained attendants around here," I told her. "Besides, Mrs. Beesaddle is in the hospital."

"Yes, so I heard," came gravely. "And under the circumstances I suppose we'll just have to get along as best we can. I dare say too that we'll come out all right if you earnestly do your part. I never could have used that first stupid boy though. Nor was I very favorably impressed with the red-headed boy either, when he answered a call this morning. I much prefer you, Jerry."

"I'll do my best to please you," I promised faithfully.

Carrying the poodles over two at a time, I was nicely stationed in my new quarters by eight-thirty, though at first I felt terribly foolish there. I felt like a girl playing with her dolls. But I had a job to perform, so grimly went at it, brushing the dogs in turn and otherwise caring for them and guarding them as instructed.

One of my firmest orders had been *never* to let the poodles walk in the dirt, though it would be perfectly all right, I had been told, to let them romp on the clean lawn. So that's were I put in the most of my time, having some dandy fun there, as Peg had predicted, for smarter dogs I never had seen. They certainly didn't deserve to be ribboned up and trimmed up so ridiculously. It made them look like clowns. Evidently though that was the style with poodles.

The camp was soon agog over Mrs. Hinds' fine clothes and jewelry. Diamonds flashed on nearly every finger. She had a triple string of pearls, too, that must have cost her a fortune. Everything about her told of great wealth and high position

—and yet something inside of me kept saying: "Watch her, Jerry! Watch her!"

At nine-thirty the hospital phoned that Mrs. Bee-saddle was still in a coma. Peg took the word around to the guests, Mrs. Clarabel later driving off to look at some more antiques and get the day's food supplies. Shortly after she drove out, Doc Leland drove in for another look at his patient, finding her sitting up crocheting.

"What did you tell me her name is, Jerry?" he stopped to ask me on the way out.

"Mrs. Hannah Topple," I told him.

"Humph!" he screwed up his forehead reflectively. "I can't git over the idear that I've seen that woman some place. That wrinkled face of hers certainly strikes me familiar. Maybe though it's jest my imagination. But what are you doing here, Jerry? Are you working here this summer?"

"I'm poodle tender extraordinary to her highness Mrs. Hetty Hinds the third," I gave him Peg's big lingo, getting a blank stare in return.

"Heh? What's that? What did you say?"

"I'm taking care of some valuable poodles for a rich woman here," I made it simpler.

"Valuable poodles, eh? Is that one of 'em over there by that little house?"

"Yes, that's Morning Gold," I laughed. "There are five more inside, named Gladiator, Whirlwind, Petsy-Patsy, Just Me and Takes-the-Cake."

Disgust flooded Doc's swarthy honest face.

"Humph!" he grunted. "I hope I never git rich, if I've got to fiddle away my time with silly shave-tailed dogs with names like that. But I guess you git plenty of people of that type here, from what I've heard about the place. Well, I'll have to be movin' on with my pills and powders to further ease humanity's ills. If Mrs. Topple should happen to need me again, give me a ring."

Mrs. Hinds put in the most of the morning playing bridge with her neighbors. I had expected her to pop in on me every half hour or so to check up on me, but having turned the poodles over to me she seemed perfectly willing to leave their care entirely up to me. The only other time I saw her that morning was when she went in to dinner with the others.

And, boy, was *that* a dress parade! Um-um! The other women weren't going to be put in the shade by the dressy newcomer, each getting out the very best she had, with jewelry to match. Ordinarily the table talk was mostly about the pets there and what beautiful weather it was—but today the talk was all about expensive trips to Paris, and how beautiful the Sphinx looked in the golden Egyptian sunset—only the camel that Mrs. Clarabel had had to ride that day shook out her lower false teeth or something like that, thus spoiling the trip for her. And Bagdad!—oh, there was the spot of spots for you, with its Oriental glamour (whatever that was!) and prevalent mysticism. I didn't get to hear it first-hand, but I could imagine from what was told me later how funny it was. Mrs. Hinds herself just put in an occasional, "Yes, that *is* a pretty spot—I remember it well," or, "Yes, my husband and I touched there in our yacht on our honeymoon."

The noon meal itself and the later planned business meeting took up almost an hour and a half, so it was well along toward two before the help got around to eat.

"Well, Jerry, we're soon going to have a show here," Peg told me, when we finally gathered around our own little table in the kitchen. "Mrs. Clarabel started the ball rolling this noon—after she got back from Egypt! They're going to build a stage in the barn and seats and everything."

"Including a balcony for Romeo, huh?" I laughed.

"No, Jerry, Romeo got only one vote. It would be nice, they all said politely, to stage one of Miss Martow's old productions, but to put on a play like that would take all summer. So it was decided to put on a radio play instead, with a regular microphone and loud speaker. We may even get in the play ourselves before they get through."

"Oh, boy, what soup!" guzzled Red, on his side.

"That's an idea, Red!" laughed Peg. "We'll use you for sound effects—when the ship sinks."

"Aye, aye, sir!" Red crazily saluted with his soup spoon.

"But what makes you think *we* may get in the play?" I asked Peg interested.

"Miss Garton told me so, just before she went out. She's going to write the play herself. It's going to be about some poor kids in an orphanage. Myrtle could have been in it, too, if she hadn't skinned out—for they need a girl like her. Boy, I still can't figure out why she skinned out that way last night! I sometimes wonder if she isn't loony."

"Has anything new happened in number eight?" I quizzed eagerly.

"No, but I can tell you something about the Captain," Peg waggled.

"What?" I asked quickly.

"He was up watching us last night when we were running around down there in the cabin row."

"His little monkey was watching us—I noticed it —but I never noticed him."

"Of course you didn't—he was standing back out of sight.   But he saw everything that was going on. Mrs. Blakeley let it drop when I stopped there with her morning paper.   We awakened her, too, it seems, and she looked out just in time to see the Captain slipping out next door with his revolver."

"Well, anyway," I said, "we know now what the number eight woman looks like without her goggles, for she was too sick last night to think of hiding her face.   Doc Leland declares he's met her some place before, but can't remember where."

"Did he tell you that, Jerry?" came eagerly.

"Yes."

"That's queer," pursued Peg, his eyes puzzled. "I have the same feeling—that I've met her some place else, too.   If I could just remember where, I think we'd have the answer to the riddle."

Red and Horse Foot were matching pennies across the table.

"Remember," said Red, with a wink at us, "heads I win and tails you lose."

"What are you two matching for?" asked Peg.

"To see who gathers up the dirty dishes.   Oh-oh! It's tails—you lose, unlucky."

The big gyp!   Horse Foot though never caught on, but patiently started with a tray to clear the

tables, Mrs. Hinds at the same time honking to me
from the drive.

"Where are my dogs, Jerry?" she asked crisply,
when I ran out.

"I locked them in the poodle parlor while I was
eating," I told her.

"Well, let me have them right away as I'm going
for a drive with them."

The poodles must have heard and understood,
for the instant the door was opened out they bounded
and across to the open car.

"You may go, too, Jerry, if you wish," I was in-
vited. "However that isn't necessary, if you have
other work to do."

"Then I think I'll stay and help the other fellows
with the dishes," I told her.

She singled out one of the poodles anxiously.

"Why!—what's the matter with Gladiator?" she
asked. "His eyes aren't right. They have a dull
look. Jerry, have you been feeding the dogs
candy?"

"No, ma'am," I declared honestly.

"Did you let them drink out of that fountain?"
came the next sharp inquiry.

"No, ma'am. I got them some water from the
spring-house where our milk is kept."

"From the spring-house?" she repeated, stiffen-
ing. "Was it spring water?"

"Yes, ma'am. That's where we get all our drinking water."

"Out of an open spring?" she still stared.

"Yes, ma'am."

"Goodness me! What a primitive system!" she

made a wry face. "I don't see how you can get intelligent people to stay here, as anything from a beetle to a rat could easily fall into an open spring. You can have some bottled water sent out from town for me. I don't want you to give any more of that spring water to my dogs either, unless you boil it. I don't trust open springs."

When she was gone I ran in and told Peg.

"Oh, she's crazy!" he growled. "There couldn't anything get into that spring—with that big wall around it. But if she wants bottled water I'll get her bottled water—and, boy, she'll pay for it, too!"

Horse Foot came singing with some more dirty dishes.

"Oh, bury me out on the l-l-lone prairie-e-e!" he murdered it.

"We'll bury you out back of the barn with the rest of the trash," threatened Peg, "if you don't quit torturing your larynx. I could make better music than that with an old squeaky shoe."

"W-w-what size?" grinned Horse Foot.

"And let me tell you something else, double discord!" Peg further fiercely went at him. "The next time you hear anybody on the roof, wake me up. If you'd done that last night we wouldn't have got caught that way. I would have known right off myself that it was the Strickers."

We were just finishing our work when Mrs. Hinds came back about three-thirty.

"Remember," she told me firmly, when I ran out to take over the poodles again, "you absolutely *must not* give them any more of that unboiled spring water. Is that clear to you?"

"Yes, ma'am," I replied.

The dogs were all out now except Gladiator himself, who lay on the back seat. I thought, and she did, too, till I touched him, that he was sleeping there. But he wasn't. He was dead!

CHAPTER XVI

THE EMPTY GRAVE

Mrs. Clarabel pussy-footed in while we were soberly doing the supper dishes.

"Is it true," she asked, her eyes dilated, "that you boys fished a dead rat out of the spring this afternoon?"

"Why, of course not," Peg snorted, angry over the talk that was going around about the spring since the death of Mrs. Hinds' poodle.

"Well," the visitor swished her head in her authoritative way, "I agree with Mrs. Hinds that we're all running grave risks drinking water out of an open spring, and shall insist on bottled water myself during the remainder of my stay here."

"Very well," conceded Peg patiently. "We'll discontinue the spring water then and use only bottled water from now on. Anything to please you, Mrs. Piper. I think, though, that Mrs. Hinds is unfair in blaming her dog's death onto the spring, and making up such bad stories about it. It's one of the best and safest springs in this section."

After Mrs. Clarabel, the Cookbook Woman anxiously slipped in.

"Is it true," she began, with a squeamish look, "that you boys found a——"

"No," Peg cut her off, grim now, "we didn't fish a dead rat out of the spring this afternoon, nor a dead cat nor a dead hippopotamus nor anything else. It's all a made-up story of Mrs. Hinds'—and I wish she'd keep her mouth shut."

"Well," came stiffly, "you needn't get impertinent about it. Certainly there must be some foundation to her story. *She* says it's the spring water that killed her poodle. I agree with her, too, that open springs are dangerous."

"Well, maybe they are," Peg refused to argue the matter further. "I've already promised Mrs. Piper to keep a supply of bottled water on hand, so you won't have anything more to worry about."

"But what if one of my cats should get some of the spring water by accident?"

Which was more than Peg could stand.

"Then we'll have some Chinaman on the other side pull the bottom of the spring out. Does that suit you?"

The woman stiffened like a poker.

"You can make out my bill," she snapped, her eyes flashing. "I'll be leaving inside of an hour. For there *are* reputable resorts around here where guests do not have to put up with impertinence and have the very lives of their pets endangered by contaminated drinking water."

"Oh, please don't go, Miss Cane!" Peg then began to beg, frantic. "I'm sorry I said that. But, gosh, I'm just about crazy. I'll do anything I can do to please you, if you'll just stay. Please, Miss Cane!"

But off she went at eight with her carful of cats, evidently headed for the near-by hotel.

I never had seen Peg more wilted.

"Jerry, this looks to me like the beginning of the

end," he told me despairingly. Then he started dancing furiously. "But, doggone it," he yelled, "no one can say I haven't tried! I've never worked so hard in all my life. The cards were all stacked against me, I guess. And that lazy old Mr. Beesaddle! If he wanted to keep the farm going, why didn't he stay here and help? He's been gone two days now. Gosh all Friday, I can't do everything alone!"

Poor old Peg! If I had sympathized with him I honestly believe he would have burst into tears— an unheard of thing for him!

The poodles were all with their hysterical owner now—she wouldn't trust them any longer with me. So at bedtime I turned in with the others in the dormitory.

We had drawn straws to see who would be next-up in case of an emergency call and having drawn the unlucky straw, I sleepily piled out when the buzzer went off at one and ran to see what was wanted.

Ten minutes later I was back shaking Peg.

"This place is getting absolutely cuckoo," I told him dizzily, when I finally got him awake.

"What's the matter now?" he asked anxiously.

"I just got an emergency call—but there's nobody up over there."

"You're sure you didn't dream it?" he looked up at the buzzer.

"Dream it—nothing! I was up and dressing before the crazy thing stopped rattling."

"But everything was dark over there, huh?" he asked further, with growing anxiety.

"Dark and still, both—like a tomb," I told him.

"I listened at all the doors—but I couldn't hear a thing."

He got up white.

"Gosh!—do you suppose it was Mrs. Topple, with a bullet in her?"

Dressed, he took me back with him on the run, tapping on her door.

"Mrs. Topple!" he called anxiously. "Oh, Mrs. Topple! Are you all right?"

There was a prompt stir inside.

"Oh, go back to bed, you idiot!" came sharply from within. "Of course I'm all right."

Peg's relief was so great that he almost collapsed.

"That's one time," he laughed weakly, "when I enjoyed being called an idiot. Boy, was I ever glad to hear *her* voice! Well, I suppose we'll have to tap on all the doors now. Let's hope we don't get a shoe pitched at us."

The Hideaway Woman came out on her porch as we started off.

"Oh, is that you, Peg?" she asked quickly, in an entirely different voice, peering at us through her screen.

"Yes, ma'am," he told her, stopping.

"I thought it was someone else. But what's the matter? Why did you wake me up?"

He explained.

"Well, it wasn't me that called," she declared, going back inside.

Nor was it any of the others, we learned, returning puzzled to the dormitory.

"I wonder who Mrs. Topple thought we were?" I curiously asked Peg, as I got back into bed.

"That's just what I've been wondering myself Jerry. Idiot, huh?" he studied. "It must be some one she knows pretty well. Say! I believe I've got it! I bet a cookie she thought it was Myrtle But what can be the tie there? Boy, it's just one tangle after another, isn't it, Jerry? But I'm going to forget about it myself and go to sleep. Let's hope we're still alive at breakfast. Good-night!"

At seven we were all up again, Peg getting dressed and out first.

"Hey, Jerry!" he called outside. "Did you know your bike's out here?"

I ran out.

"I never left it out here," I told him. "It was locked inside when we went to sleep last night Someone's been using it, too!"

"Yes, and here's an old postcard tucked under the seat," he made the discovery.

"The scenery here is wonderful—especially in the moonlight," the crumpled picture-card read. "I do a lot of riding on a borrowed bicycle, belonging to a boy with sore feet. I think I know now what gave me those mysterious headaches—but please do not worry or wonder about me."

That was all!—and at first we didn't get any sense out of it. When we came to study it though, for hidden meanings, we got a lot of sense out of it.

It was from Myrtle of course! In some unknown way she had worked the dormitory buzzer to get us up so that she could slip in unnoticed and get one of our bikes. *The scenery here is wonderful— especially in the moonlight.* That meant she had been out near by doing something of importance to her in the moonlight. (But what?) *"I do a lot of riding on a borrowed bike, belonging to a boy with sore feet."* The part about the *"feet"* was just put in so we'd know for sure who had been using the bike—*"a lot of riding"* would mean a long trip and probably a very necessary one. (But to where?—and to what ends?) Her *"mysterious headache"* was the mystery itself (a headache to a good many of us, if you ask me!)—all apparently clear to her now. Evidently more bewildering things were to follow, too, for we were told *"not to worry or wonder."*

Mrs. Hinds came in to phone while the others were at breakfast. Over and over again she told whoever was on the wire with her about the contaminated spring water killing her poodle, the other guests plainly stretching their ears to hear as much as they could.

"Is that bottled water?" Mrs. Clarabel inquired squeamishly, when I came around to fill her tumbler.

"Yes, ma'am," I assured. "We had it brought in early this morning."

Mrs. Hinds kept on at the phone in a loud voice.

"Why, of course, it was the spring water that killed my poodle," she declared. "What else could it have been? You can tell by the tubercular look of the cattle here that the water isn't pure. We've actually been drinking it ourselves, too—and heaven only knows how many dead rats have been slyly fished out of it behind our backs."

Mrs. Clarabel was up now white-faced, her handkerchief to her lips.

"Oh, dear!" came biliously. "I think I'll go back to my cabin."

"Yes, the actress similarly got up, "I think I'll go back to my cabin, too."

Still Mrs. Hinds went it at the phone.

"No, I haven't any thought of suing them here over my loss, though I could, as I'm satisfied myself that the drainage here is just as unsanitary as the water supply. I'll probably get out of here with the others before the day is over. Certainly I don't want to lose any more of my pets here."

The actress checked out peakedly with her parrot at nine-thirty, with the lame excuse that she had to hurry back to the city to start rehearsals for a new play. After her, at ten, went Mrs. Blakeley with Whoopee, and finally at ten-thirty, Mr. and Mrs. Clarabel, antiques hanging from every corner of their car, the inside crammed to the top with bird cages, cats and dogs. Mr. Clarabel himself didn't want to go. He was still growling about it, with longing looks back, when the loaded car disappeared into the highway.

When night set in we were shivering in our shoes, for on top of everything else the carcass of the dead dog had now disappeared. Following its death we had been asked to bury it carefully in some pretty quiet spot, but when Mrs. Hinds went out for a final look at the expected mound, before leaving herself, all she found there was an empty hole. Overnight the carcass had been exhumed and mysteriously spirited off.

Strangely Mrs. Hinds stayed on after that, quizzing us over and over again about the empty grave.

But if *we* hadn't dug the carcass up, who had? Surely we must know something about it, she persisted. Our inability to clear up the mystery for her seemed to frighten her more than distress her.

Peg desperately phoned the hospital at eight that night to try and persuade Mr. Beesaddle to come home and take charge of things, as the farm's business was almost at a standstill now. With Mrs. Topple still having her meals brought to her and the Captain supposedly doing the cooking, there were only three guests in to the last meal, Mrs. Hinds herself and the two women in number three.

"Is Mr. Beesaddle coming back tonight?" I eagerly asked Peg, when he returned from the phone.

"No, Jerry," came downcast. "He's sick himself now—from worrying over his wife, I guess. She's worse, too. They're going to operate on her tonight. Oh, gee! I guess we'll just have to stick till the ship finally sinks."

Red ran to the door as a pair of headlights turned in.

"Here comes a car, fellows," he cried. "Maybe it's a customer."

But it wasn't—it was the county health officer, come to inspect our spring.

"Um," he looked it over carefully, as Peg and I stood anxiously by. "Seems like a thoroughly satisfactory spring to me."

"Who said it wasn't?" Peg asked bluntly.

"One of your own guests here, for one. I've had three calls altogether about it today."

"Well, I can't imagine who'd call besides Mrs. Hinds," growled Peg bewildered. "She's got the crazy idea that the water killed one of her dogs—she's even been telling that we fished a dead rat out of the spring. But it's all a lie."

The health officer listened attentively to the whole story.

"Do you know what I think, boys?" he spoke gravely, when Peg concluded.

"What?" Peg asked eagerly.

"I wouldn't want you to repeat this—but it looks to me as though there's some kind of a hidden scheme on foot here to ruin your summer's business. Who is this Mrs. Hinds anyway?—has she ever been here before?"

"Not that I know of," replied Peg.

"Is she still here?"

"Yes, sir."

"If I were you I'd find some quick way of getting rid of her, before she drives off the rest of your guests. Mind, though, that you don't bring my name into it. I'll take some of the water back to the laboratory for analysis, though I can't conceive that there's anything the matter with it, unless the spring has been tampered with. We'll know though when I get back to the laboratory. What's your phone number?"

Peg gave it.

"Well, I'll give you a ring in a couple of hours, for I'm going to get at the bottom of this matter as quickly as possible. How is Mrs. Beesaddle to-night?"

"Pretty bad," Peg reported long-faced.

"She's a grand woman, boys," we were told earnestly. "I was brought up around here and I know.   She's deserving of anything any of us can do to help her."

Peg dug at his hair.

"Do you actually believe, mister," he asked intently, "that Mrs. Hinds was sent here purposely to kill our business?"

"It certainly looks like it to me," came the grave reply.

"But how about her dead dog?"

"She could have poisoned it herself as part of the plot."

Back came Peg's old fighting look with a rush.

"That's exactly what she did do," he grated, his eyes flashing over the unfairness and cruelty of it. "And I thought she was such a grand woman!   Remember what I told you about her, Jerry?—I said, no, don't suspect *her!*   A dog poisoner!   Of all the low tricks!   She probably poisoned the poor dog after she took it out with her yesterday in her car, letting you think at first, Jerry, that it was asleep on the back seat.   Then she made all that fuss about the spring water!   Why, of course, that's it!" Peg's excitement grew, as he ran on.   "Look what she told everybody!   And when she phoned this morning!—she just did it so the other guests would hear her.   Then this afternoon!—when she found the dead dog gone!   Don't you see why she was so scared, Jerry?   That dog was full of poison and she was scared stiff that whoever took it was wise to her scheme and intended exposing her.   But who *did* take it?" came puzzled.   "And who's behind the scheme?   What's your opinion, Jerry?"

Red came running before I could answer.

"Where's Mrs. Hinds?" he cried excitedly. "Someone wants her on the phone, but I can't find her."

"Isn't she in her cabin?" asked Peg.

"No. The dogs are there, and her car's in front. But I can't find her."

CHAPTER XVII

A WILD NIGHT

AT TEN-THIRTY the health officer phoned that his sample of our drinking water had tested as nearly one hundred per cent pure as any natural drinking water from any source could. So it wasn't a case of the spring being tampered with by some enemy of the farm's, as he had thought possible, but purely a case of lying on the part of Mrs. Hinds.

Nor were we long in deciding who had sent her there. It was that runtish hotel manager of course! Considering that a nice dog had been cruelly sacrificed to the scheme, and that it had been carried on when the worthy farm owners were least able to protect themselves against it, it seemed to us about the lowest scheme imaginable. It was hard for us to believe that people of any class or type, even hardened criminals, could do a thing like that. The woman was so pretty, too!—and so nice to talk to!

Well, the wreckage of the summer business there showed how effective the scheme had been. Four cabins stood completely empty, with only the five dogs in a fifth. The dogs themselves seemed to sense that something was wrong, whining piteously whenever we looked in on them. Finally we removed them to the farmhouse, satisfied now that the guilty owner, fearing the consequences of her treachery, had abandoned them. But why had she gone off without her car? That to us was one of the biggest riddles of all.

There really was nothing we could do there now expect to rebuild our fences, as the saying is, and get along as best we could, hoping that the damaging reports about our water supply and sanitation would soon die down. In time maybe we would have the cabins filled with desirable renters again. When the true story got around, we might even get some of those back who had just left so panicky, as there always had been a lot of genuine enjoyment there before the combined effect of Mrs. Beesaddle's absence and the damaging scheme began to tell on the place.

Instead of being the professional dog exhibitor she had pretended, Mrs. Hinds (or whatever her real name was) probably was just a clever unscrupulous crook in the knavish hotel manager's employ. Probably the dogs now left with us weren't nearly as valuable either as had been told. No wonder she had quizzed me that way to learn if there were any other professional exhibitors there! If there had been it wouldn't have been so easy for her to continue her pose. But what had become of the carcass of the dead dog? Had Myrtle herself taken the dead dog away to some poison expert, to verify certain suspicions of hers?

The night she ran off she evidently had just feared that something bad for the farm was liable to happen, without then having a very clear idea what. In her later postcard though she had said: *"I think I know now what gave me those mysterious head-*

aches," which plainly meant that now she *knew* the nature of the plot afoot.

But whatever her suspicions or later movements had been, why in the world, we asked each other, hadn't she confided in us, to get our help? Why did she feel she had to work alone that way? Was it just a silly notion? She had cried in leaving, saying she didn't want to leave but had to. Just what did she mean by that?"

This all had happened, too, on the heels of the Poodle Woman's arrival. Plainly Myrtle, recognizing the woman, had kept out of her sight, sending Horse Foot to show her to her cabin. Later we had been asked to turn out the light—Myrtle telling us that she feared harmful outside eyes. That could mean only the Poodle Woman, though we had had other scattered ideas at the time. Myrtle evidently, too, had feared that the Poodle Woman, in prowling about, might find the bike postcard ahead of us—hence the attempt to make it appear like a harmless card from someone at a pleasure resort.

There were any number of things that we could put together now—but we still couldn't figure out why Myrtle had felt she had to work alone that way, under cover of night, and why she was in such deadly fear of the Poodle Woman.

One thing, we were satisfied that the other mystery there, involving the Hideaway Woman and Captain Danglers (and possibly Myrtle, too), had nothing to do with the plot to wreck the farm's summer business. Both the Captain and Mrs. Topple were indignant when told of the plot and its result, as also were the two women in number three. There were some things to learn there yet, but it was nothing to worry about.

With the Poodle Woman gone, we partly looked for Myrtle back before bedtime, as she couldn't be far off. But at eleven there was still no sign of her, and determined to get a little fun out of our jobs there, instead of just worry and bewilderment, we loaded ourselves down with pails and a sheet and started in a rowboat to pay a call on the Strickers.

Passing the old Windmere hotel, a jagged black outline against the night sky, we came finally to the lighted Woodlawn Bay hotel pier and quietly got out.

Peg had had several phone calls from one of the kitchenmaids here—it seems she was a cousin of his or something (anyway that's what he told us!)— and through her he had learned that the Strickers, like us, had a whole detached cabin to themselves. There were four of these "help" cabins in all, Peg had been told, and the Strickers were in number three.

We were pretty sure, from the activity around the hotel, that the Strickers were still on duty somewhere, but first crept up on the darkened cabin to make certain.

"Are you sure this is the right cabin?" I asked Peg, in a whisper, as we listened at the open door.

"Sure thing. Rosie said number three. She's in number one herself, with some other girls. She said there's a big fat pastry cook in number two. I don't know who is in number four—but that doesn't matter. This is the cabin we're interested in.

Seems all quiet in there, too.   Has anybody got the sheet?"

"Sure—I've got it," I told him eagerly.

"Well, listen, Jerry!—you go in now and hide under one of the beds, as we planned.   When the Strickers come in they'll probably lock themselves in, which is why I'm sending you in ahead.   All right! You just lay there, out of sight, till they're ready to drop off—you know, half awake and half asleep. In the meantime we'll stretch our rope across the door and have our water buckets ready.   Then out from under the bed comes the ghost—meaning you, see!—and out the scared Strickers go through the door and down in a heap.   We're going to get the dirtiest water we can find, too, and boy, will they get a ducking while they're down!   But you better get inside now, Jerry!   Good luck!"

I found two big beds inside, both empty yet, and quickly getting away back under one of them I began my wait.

It got kind of tiresome—it was terribly stuffy under there, too.   But the thought of the fun that was to follow kept me spurred up.

Presently someone came in heavily and turned on the light.   But it wasn't one of the expected Strickers.   It was a woman!   It was that big fat pastry cook that Peg had mentioned.   And she started right off to get ready for bed.

Gee-miny-crickets-gosh-all-Friday!   WOUGH!

To this day I don't know whether Rosie purposely gave Peg the wrong number as a joke, or whether we had started counting the cabins from the wrong end of the row. But there I was unmistakably under the cook's bed. Boy, did I sweat!

First she took off her shoes and stockings, thus bringing into sight two of the biggest feet that I ever had seen on any living thing except a full-grown elephant. I didn't waste any time looking at those feet though. I realized that I had to get out of there, and get out blamed quick. And unable to think of a better plan I filled my lungs to capacity and let out the awfullest screechiest cat yowl that anybody had heard since the beginning of time— figuring it would send her flying for the open, thus giving me my chance to escape.

But it didn't work that way. Instead of flying out screeching in fear herself, she bent down and peeped wide-eyed under the bed.

"Boo!" I went at her, shoving my sheet into her fat face. This time she did leg it, those big feet of hers going FLOP, FLOP, FLOP, like a pair of snow shovels.

She was still legging it in the general direction of the equator when I got out—Peg and the others then starting to laugh their heads off at me.

"Oh, boy!" Peg whooped it up, in his glee over my mortification. "Wait till Mamma Todd hears about her model son hiding under a fat lady's bed. Shameful! Shameful!"

"Listen!" I went at him fiercely, my face and neck burning. "If you ever dare to tell anybody about this, you pie-eyed, squash-head, I'll lay you down so hard the buzzards will start nibbling on you."

Then of course Red had to get in some of *his* smartness!—the big baboon-face!

THIS TIME SHE DID LEG IT.

"An honor Scout, too!" he tush-tushed, with a pretended horrified air. "Wait till our Scoutmaster hears about this!"

"And what I told Peg goes for you, too, you gabby imitation of a cockeyed cockroach," I furiously turned on him. "If you ever dare to tell anybody about this I'll kick your shins so hard you'll think you're wearing woodpeckers for garters."

"He sure talks hard, doesn't he, Red?" tittered Peg.

"Yes," similarly tittered Red, "he thinks he's Big Stuff now, since he's got to be a bed-hider-under."

Horse Foot was running around peeping into the bushes.

"W-w-where's the cat?" he queried.

"Yes, Jerry," Peg giggled in again, "was that a real cat that we heard, or was it you vocalizing?"

"None of your business," I told him.

"Anyway," tittered Red, "that's one way to coo to your soul mate! Meow-w!"

Horse Foot was still peeping.

"B-b-but where's the cat?" he persisted.

"Oh, go on down and get in the boat and shut up," I told him, starting off myself.

"But we aren't going home yet!" Peg spoke hastily, holding back.

"I am," I told him flatly.

"Oh, rats!" he growled, taking in unwillingly after us. "You would spoil everything, you big sissy."

"Who's a big sissy?" I faced him, my jaw squared.

"You are," he growled, his own jaw squared.

"Quit your fighting—you two!" Red put in hastily. "For here comes the manager. Jiggers, all of you!"

It was harder rowing going back, as we had the current to buck.

"Well, sorehead!" Peg grinned at me in the moonlight, as he tugged at the oars. "Are you still mad? You can't take anything, can you?"

"But, gosh!" I squirmed, "who wants to have a story like that get out about them! Mother *would* be ashamed of me if she ever heard that—there's no joke about it either. Honest, now," I begged, "you fellows won't tell on me, will you? Please!"

"It's hard to keep still when you know anything as funny as that," tittered Peg.

"And, how!" chimed in Red.

I saw then that the only thing to do was to laugh it off myself, as I should have done at the start. After all, it *was* funny, as they said. And those big feet! Oh-oh! Red almost tumbled out of the boat laughing when I told him about them—and how I went "Boo!" in the woman's face.

Hearing voices up ahead somewhere, Peg slowed up. Then we caught sight of a light from the direction of the old Windmere hotel. A fire there lit up a large spot in the woods.

"Do you suppose the place is burning down?" Peg wondered anxiously.

Red stood up for a better look.

"No," he told us, "it isn't anything burning down. It's someone burning something in that old fireplace that still stands there."

The walls that once had shut in the big living

room fireplace were all down now, as was the floor
of the above rooms and the roof. The fireplace
stood all alone. We had noticed it before, but
couldn't imagine who'd be using it at that time of
night.

Curious, we pulled up and quietly got out to see,
learning, when we got closer, that it was the very
gang we were after! Having gotten off duty earlier than we had expected, here they were, all four
of them, gathered in front of the roaring fireplace,
with only the sky over them, toasting marshmallows
and crazily singing pirate songs. Oh, boy! Oh,
boy! Were we ever in luck! All we had to do
now was to get some suitable ammunition and pepper them—for they stood out like actors on an open
stage.

Horse Foot in landing had clumsily stepped
ankle-deep into some firm sticky mud and filling our
buckets with this, we crept back, getting up to within
a few yards of them—then, all rising together with
a wild whoop, we let fly.

"*Ouch!*" squawked Bid the leader, as I took him
on the back of the head with my first beautifully
aimed mud ball. "Someone's pegging mud at us!"

"It's Jerry Todd!" Jimmy Stricker ducked shriek-
ing, the mud balls flying all around him. Then he
got a lulu right in the bread basket. "*Ouch!*" he
gurgled, doubling up.

At the same time Jum and Chet were getting it
right and left. Spat, spat, spat! At every "spat"
there was a loud painful squawk. Bid tried at the
start to get his gang organized to fight back, but
soon decided that the safest thing for him was to

flee, so off he went, the others squawking behind him, the mud balls still flying after them.

Chasing them through the moonlit woods clear over to their own hotel and peppering them from head to foot, we then went back laughing and talking to feast ourselves on the remaining marshmallows. There had been a big bag there when the Strickers were driven off, but when we got there the bag was gone. The fire, too, looked as though someone had poured water on it.

Could it be that Myrtle, hiding there somewhere, had gotten the marshmallows ahead of us? We ran through the roofless rooms calling her name, getting only a ghostly mournful owl hoot in reply.

It was twelve when we finally turned in, and seven when we were out again the next morning. Breakfast over, we went about our various jobs as usual, the county sheriff coming in about nine to question us about the vanished Poodle Woman.

It seems she hadn't run off at all, as we had thought, but had disappeared right there on our own farm. That was why her car was still there.

CHAPTER XVIII

THE PICTURE IN THE NEWSPAPER

THE sheriff's visit gave us something more to wonder about. Had Mrs. Hinds really been put out of the way for some unknown reason, and her body secreted somewhere on the farm? The sheriff's grim actions, as he poked about in the buildings and straw piles, suggested it. His pointed questions suggested, too, that he thought we had had a part in the disappearance.

We were glad when he finally left.

Dad dropped in next on his way to Ashton, the county seat, eight miles farther east.

"What's back of all these stories that I've been hearing about your farm, Jerry?" he asked gravely. "Did you boys really poison one of the valuable dogs here?"

I gave him the straight of it.

"But where did the sheriff get the idea that you boys were responsible for the Poodle Woman's disappearance?" he asked next.

"I don't know," I shrugged.

"Didn't you ask him?"

"Sure thing—but he wouldn't tell us."

"Did he find any trace of the woman in his search of the premises?"

"Not that I know of."

I'd never seen Dad's face longer.

"I'm half inclined to take you home with me, son," he decided.

"Why?" I asked quickly.

"I'm afraid to leave you here any longer. I'm afraid something may happen to you. People don't disappear that way without a reason, and I'd hate to learn, after you had disappeared, too, that there *was* some strange deadly peril hanging over the place. You say yourself that you half suspect it."

"Yes, but that's just our own idea, Dad," I made light of it to him, to get to stay if I could. "And I don't think the sheriff had any real proof that the Poodle Woman disappeared here, or he would have said so."

"But you say her car's still here, and that's proof in itself, Jerry, that she disappeared here."

"Not necessarily," I argued. "Maybe she had to leave in a hurry and couldn't get her car started. Maybe she lost her keys. Or maybe she *wanted* to leave her car here."

"But why should she want to leave in such a hurry?"

"Because we had found her out, and knew what she was up to. If she didn't hurry off, she knew she'd be arrested. So away she went on the fly to save herself. That's our idea."

"Did you boys talk this way to the sheriff?"

"Sure thing."

"But he still kept to the idea that she was right here on the farm, huh?"

"Y-yes, I guess so," I had to admit.

"Which looks to me, Jerry," Dad followed that up, "as though the sheriff is a whole lot better informed on what's been going on here in the background than any of you boys. Did he say at any time that he had come here to arrest the woman?"

"No," I shook my head.

"Did he say that she had a prison record?"

"No."

"Well, there's certainly some deep mystery about this," Dad concluded, completely puzzled himself.

"Yes, and that's exactly why I want to stay," I told him eagerly. "Please let me, Dad! I've solved other mysteries, and I think I can solve this one, too, if you'll let me."

My eagerness seemed to amuse him.

"Well," he partly gave in, with a chummy half smile at me, "I think I'll have a little talk with the sheriff myself when I get to Ashton. I'll know then whether or not it's safe to leave you here."

Later he phoned the astonishing information from the county seat that the man who had been there that morning, calling himself the sheriff, wasn't the real sheriff at all, but an impostor. And there the mystery stood, with us all on edge and expectant, when another night came.

Supper over, and the work done up, we went into the lighted office to wait for calls.

"What are you studying about?" I asked Peg, as we stood together in the doorway watching the deepening darkness outside. "You look as solemn as an old owl."

"I wish I was as wise as an old owl," he rejoined gravely.

"I've heard that owls are stupid," I told him.

"They just look wise. But what's on your mind anyway?—the Strickers?"

"Why should I waste time thinking about them?" he grumbled.

"I thought maybe you were thinking up some scheme to turn the tables on them, if they should decide to pay us another visit tonight. They're probably still smarting over what we gave them last night, and itching to get even. It'll pay us to be on our guard, Peg."

"Oh, let the Strickers go—we can easily take care of them if they show up," he dismissed them impatiently. "What's worrying me is that man who passed himself off on us as the sheriff this morning. Have you been able to figure out, Jerry, who he was and what his object was in poking around here that way?"

"He was searching for Mrs. Hinds—so he said."

"And you actually believe that, huh?" Peg gave me a quiet curious look.

"Well, that's what he told us," I shrugged.

"He told us that he was the sheriff, too, but we know now that he wasn't. So maybe he was lying about the other, too. Maybe it wasn't Mrs. Hinds at all that he was searching for. Maybe it was something entirely different."

"What, for instance?" I asked eagerly.

"That's what I'd like to know myself," Peg spoke gravely, his eyes still fastened on the disappearing world outside. "That's why I say I wish I was as wise as an old owl. I'd feel a whole lot safer, Jerry, if I knew exactly what was going on around here in the background. You know, we have a lot of ideas. We have ideas about the Hideaway Woman and the Captain. We have ideas about her going to the cemetery that way, with him after her. We have ideas about Myrtle, too, and why she had to skin out so mysteriously that night. We have a lot of ideas about a lot of things. But have you stopped to think how little we really know? We don't even know for sure that Mrs. Hinds poisoned her dog. Jerry," his intenseness grew, "there may be something going on out there in the dark that would knock us cuckoo if we knew about it. The thought of it almost staggers me. I'm no calf. But when I fight something I want to be able to see it and know what I'm fighting. I wish it was morning."

I ran out here to answer a call from number eight, the Hideaway Woman telling me to get a set of dominoes, if I could, and come back for a few games with her.

It was almost ten, with the moon just weakly coming up, when I got back to the farmhouse, Horse Foot in the meantime having dropped asleep on the office floor, three of the poodles nosed up against him on one side and two on the other.

"Take a look at that!" I held up a shiny half dollar to Peg.

"Have you been playing dominoes with her all this time?" he asked, with a curious look at me.

"Sure thing. She's a nice old lady, too—I like her, now that I'm better acquainted with her. She has two grandchildren in Chicago, Busty and Dorf —a pretty lively pair, from what she told me about them. She often plays dominoes with them at home, she said. I think she was kind of homesick for them tonight—that's why she wanted to play with me. Boy, I wish I could get fifty cents every day for playing dominoes. That's an easy way to make money."

"Yes," Red looked up from a book, scowling, "you get the easy jobs, and I have to read to that crazy Pekingese. Thank heaven though it's gone."

"I'd be glad if it came back, and all the other dogs and cats with it," Peg said earnestly. "I'd like to see the cabins filled again, for Mrs. Beesaddle's sake."

"Did you hear anything from her today, Peg?" I asked.

"Yes, I phoned the hospital while you were dominoing. She's quite a bit better tonight, the nurse reported—and the old man, too. So there's hopes that one of them will be home soon. But what did you say the names of those grandchildren were, Jerry?" he asked intently. "Tell me again."

"Busty and Dorf," I repeated the names. "One's eleven and the other's nine. Their father is the old lady's son."

"Busty and Dorf, huh?" Peg repeated thoughtfully. "Where did I hear those names lately? It seems like it was just today, too." Then he brightened. "Oh, yes!—I remember now. There was something about them in the morning newspaper."

In his haste to get the newspaper, across the room, Peg almost wrecked poor Horse Foot, who popped up sleepily rubbing his head.

"O-o-ouch!" he squealed. "Who kicked me?"

"Never mind," purred Red. "One more kick on the head won't hurt you any."

"It was me, Horse Foot," Peg admitted, as he got the newspaper and got back to me. "Don't look so mad about it—I didn't mean to do it. Blame it onto my big feet. But if you're that sleepy, you better take your dogs and go on down to the dormitory, instead of laying there."

"What?" squeaked Red, his nose going up. "Do we have to sleep with those crazy-looking poodles tonight? They'll give us the nightmare."

"I told Horse Foot if he stayed here he'd have to take care of them," declared Peg, as he ran through the newspaper. "But keep still now, I'm looking for something."

"If it's brains," grinned Red, "you won't find it in a newspaper. You'll have to come to me. Oh, boy!—did I tell you that time! Yippee!"

The noisy egg! But that was one of the things about him that we all liked.

In following Horse Foot out, the poodles I noticed hesitated at the door as though their keen senses told them that there was something out there in the dark that wasn't good for them. Horse Foot though made them go on. I could hear him sleepily talking to them as he went down the tree-bordered path with them. Then his voice died out.

"Well, what did you find?" I asked Peg, who was still pawing through the newspaper.

"Nothing yet," he said shortly.

"What are you looking for?—the funnies?" Red asked across the room.

"No—the picture section."

"Well, why didn't you tell me—I've been sitting on it."

"Throw it over," ordered Peg.

Getting it, he pointed out a picture to me in the upper righthand corner.

"There you are, Jerry!" came triumphantly.

"But where does it give their names?" I peered.

"Under the picture—see? And over it, it says: 'Will these two happy little boys some day control the breakfast food supply of the nation?'"

I was reading myself now.

"But how can their names be Busty and Dorf Stone," I asked Peg, "if their father is Mrs. Topple's son? Wouldn't their last name be Topple, too?"

"You've got two answers to that, Jerry. Either she's had a second husband, named Topple, or that's just an assumed name to help her hide out here. But look what it says about her!" Peg's excitement grew as he read. "Gee-miny crickets, Jerry!— you've been playing dominoes with one of the richest women in the country."

"Yes, if it's really her," I spoke doubtfully.

"Of course it's her," came confidently. "The newspaper says her factories produce more than three-quarters of the world's breakfast food supply. Well, tickle my whiskers! Imagine a woman like that living here in a little one-room cabin!— and under an assumed name! For I bet you that's the situation. No wonder she had a bodyguard! Get me the guest book, Jerry—quick!"

"What guest book?" I asked.

"The book over there on the registration desk. Let me have it—I want to see it."

When I got it for him he ran through it quickly.

"I thought so," came triumphantly. "She arrived here on the evening of May twenty-second, and he came early the following morning. That proves the tie between them."

"But if he's her bodyguard, as you say, why didn't he come with her?"

Peg's black eyes were dancing now.

"Do you know what I think, Jerry?" he put his wits to work.

"What?" I asked.

"I think she skipped out, from all her rich things, just to get a nice quiet rest down here in the country. But it wouldn't do to have her going off that way unguarded. There was too much danger from kidnapers. So the son sent the guard after her whether she wanted him or not. I rather imagine, from what I've seen and heard around here, that she didn't want him. It probably nettled her when he showed up. Remember the night we tapped on her door and she called me an idiot? She thought it was him!" Peg laughed heartily here. "So that's her mystery, huh? And we were so puzzled about it! She's just a rich woman, tired of her riches, trying to get away from them, for a few weeks at least, to get a rest."

"How about that young newspaper woman?" I asked. "Where does she come in?"

"I don't know, Jerry. But it must be something about her radio plays."

"How about Myrtle?" I then asked.

"There may be a tie there," Peg considered thoughtfully. "Or it may be just some more of our imagination."

The conversation was stopped here by the thumping entrance of the bodyguard who came to make himself some coffee. Peg at the same time made all of us some sandwiches. With these down and the cabin lights out, we locked up for the night and started down the moonlit path to the dormitory.

There we found the poddles all whining at the door as they had at the farmhouse door when Horse Foot took them out. But Horse Foot himself was gone!

CHAPTER XIX

THE CAPTURE

"Did you see any sign of him, Jerry?" Peg asked me worried, when we met in front of the dormitory after a hasty search outside.

"No," I told him shortly, worried myself and scared.

Red came running from the direction of the barn.

"I just saw that man again, fellows!" he panted, his eyes popping with excitement.

"What man?" Peg demanded.

"Why, that big bruiser who was here this morning—who told us he was the sheriff."

"Where is he?" Peg asked quickly.

"I just saw him go into the barn."

"Was Horse Foot with him?"

"No."

"Are you sure, Red," pressed Peg, "that it's the same man? Did you get a good look at him?"

"I sure did," waggled Red. "He crossed right in front of me in the moonlight."

"Did he see you?"

"No—I squatted in the bushes."

"And you say he went into the barn?"

"Yes. He went through that big door in front."

"What'll we do, Jerry?" Peg turned to me for advice. "Shall we phone for the cops?"

"I think we better," I told him.

"Boy, I wish I knew where Horse Foot was," he anxiously looked around again. "This farm is a regular mystery nest. If there isn't someone disappearing, there's someone around spying. Who do you suppose that guy is, Jerry, and what do you suppose he's after?"

"Let's get the cops here before he gets away," was my answer to that.

"Yes—one of you run and phone," Peg directed. "How about you, Red? Will you go?"

I could see that Red hated to separate again.

"I guess so," he finally consented. "But where'll you be when I get back?"

"On the east side of the barn. But hurry now! And tell the cops to get here just as soon as they can."

"What'll you and I do in the meantime?" I asked Peg, as Red sped off.

"Hunt first for the man's car," came businesslike, "and yank some of his wires loose to keep him from getting away. He's the key to the whole mystery, Jerry. Now that we've got him here we've got to keep him and get someone here to capture him."

"Where do you think his car is?" I asked.

"It should be out in front or in the drive. Come on, let's see."

Finding the car in some bushes in front, just as he had expected, Peg raised the hood and gave the distributor wires a violent yank.

"There!" he chuckled, dropping the hood. "Let him get away now, if he can."

Red was running around looking for us at the barn.

"The phone's dead," he told us excitedly.

"Dead?" Peg repeated. "Are you sure?"

"I couldn't get anybody."

"But you should have kept on trying, Red. Maybe the operator was asleep."

"If you ask me," grunted Red, "I think the wires have been cut."

Here a peculiar muffled cry came from inside the barn, followed in a few seconds by what sounded to us like a groan, and then someone falling.

"What was that?" gasped Peg, staring at me.

"Don't ask me," I told him. "I've given up guessing about things around here."

"That first cry sounded to me like Horse Foot," shivered Red, looking at the barn as though he half expected it to make a lunge and grab him.

Peg started for the barn door.

"Come on, fellows," he called back, his face grim now and hard. "If that was Horse Foot we've got to go in and help him. That man may be crazy. Maybe he's got Horse Foot in there hurting him."

Red stopped at the door.

"Maybe one of us should wait outside," he quavered.

"Oh, come on!—don't be a calf!" growled Peg. "Let's stick together."

I knew exactly how Red felt. I felt the same way. I felt maybe we'd all get laid out in there. But Peg had the right idea. If Horse Foot was in there, in peril, it was our duty to help him. It was good sense for us to stick together, too.

"I wish we had a flashlight," said Peg, when we were inside.

"Shall I run back to the dormitory and get one?"
I offered.

"No, Jerry. I think we better keep going. A
little moonlight comes through the barn cracks
I'm beginning to see better already. See!—there'
the horse stalls over there."

"What's that?" I pointed in the other direction

"A pile of hay."

Something banged in back.

"What was that?" I breathed, clutching Peg'
arm.

"The door between here and the cow stable,
think."

We could hear someone coming on the run.

"Quick!" cried Peg. "Dive into the hay, fel
lows."

And did Red and I dive! Oh, boy! No panicky
groundhog ever got into its hole any quicker than we
got into that hay.

Peg came out first.

"All right, fellows. You're safe now."

"Who was it, and where did he go to?" I asked
Peg, looking around.

"I couldn't see him, Jerry. But I think he went
out the east door, where we came in, for right after
he passed us I heard the door bang."

Here a groan came faintly from in back.

"It's someone in the cow stable," gasped Red.

We all thought it was Horse Foot tied up in
there, or maybe half knocked out. But who do you
suppose we actually found when we guardedly got
there. The spy himself! Horse Foot, instead of
getting knocked out as we had thought, had knocked

the spy out, tying him hand and foot, and then running out to tell us about it.

Sure thing!—the runner who sent us diving into the hay was our own chum! He still laughs about it—the little smart aleck! He started calling me "Ostrich" too, because an ostrich, you know, runs and hides its head that way. But I soon stopped that.

When the whole story got out later, a lot of people praised Horse Foot for what he had done. They said he was a brave boy. I've never felt myself though that what he did that memorable night was a brave act. It seemed more like a foolhardy act to me—or a dumbbell act, if you want to put it that way. There was no need of him doing what he did. If he had used good sense, instead of setting out to capture the spy single-handed, he would have called on us to help him. But he didn't.

About to get into bed, he had seen the spy poking around in the moonlight. Then, as we know, the spy went into the barn. Horse Foot had anticipated that and got in there first. He had a club— almost as big as a baseball bat! Climbing onto a box just inside the stable door, he gave a cry for help, trying to make his voice sound like a woman's. The spy thought it was Mrs. Hinds—it was her that he really was searching for, as I'll explain later. He ran back when he heard the cry, thinking that his persistent search was about to be rewarded. Then, as he dashed through the stable door, down came the club on his head with perfect aim—and down he went like a log, to be later taken off to jail by the real sheriff and sentenced for his part in the conspiracy to wreck the pet farm.

It turned out that his part in the scheme was a very small one, and probably he never would have been involved in it at all if the Poodle Woman hadn't so peculiarly disappeared there. Just as we had figured out, the crooked hotel manager was back of the scheme. To his complete bewilderment the woman he had sent there suddenly disappeared. Remember the afternoon she drove off alone in her car and came back with the dead dog? She went mainly to report to him, meeting him down the road. Then between them they poisoned the poor dog! She was to have reported again that night, but didn't, and that is when he began phoning her, thus learning of her disappearance. His first thought was that she had skinned out on him. When he learned though that her car was there, he jumped to the conclusion that we had locked her up some place on the farm to keep her from telling more harmful stories about it. He didn't want her caught and questioned by the police—that would be bad for him. Nor could he come to the farm himself to search for her without arousing suspicion. So he called on a friend of his, the man passing himself off as the sheriff to make sure of getting in. Finding nothing on his first trip (he had just told us he was looking for her body to scare us and possibly get us to confess), he had been sent back, cutting the phone wires for his own protection—and you know what happened to him! They told around the jail the next day that he had a bump on his head as big as a goose egg—with Horse Foot the Hero, of course, getting the credit for it! Huh! Norning himself got safely away. They say he wound up in South America. Well, wherever he is I hope he knows now that crooked schemes like that one of his don't pay. Good business is fair business. Later the actual owner of the Woodlawn Bay hotel (a fine gallant old gentleman) came to Mrs. Beesaddle and apologized for what his manager had done. Today the new manager of the hotel and Mrs. Beesaddle are good friends, and often send each other business in rush periods.

Of course, with the spy's arrest, and Norning's flight, everybody began asking: "Where *is* the Poodle Woman?" Nor was the truth long in coming out—but I think I can best tell it by first telling Myrtle's pitiful story.

With no knowledge of her parents or why they had abandoned her shortly after her birth, she had grown up in a cheerless mismanaged orphanage, becoming finally the drudge there, and later a similar drudge in a private home in Chicago. But though her days in the city were long and hard, with poor pay, she liked it far better there, as she could attend shows there and see other girls and women doing the things on the stage that she had always longed to do. Her mind set on being a great dancer (as she had told us that day), she even entered a dancing school in the city, though her one weekly lesson took almost her whole week's pay. There she was ridiculed by the other more fortunate and prettier girls, because of her own ugly features and coarse hands. More than once, I guess, she went home in tears, but doggedly kept to her plan, finally developing a grace of movement that became the envy of those who had ridiculed her. It was in the dancing school that she met the pretty yellow-haired woman who later palmed herself off on us as the very elegant and much-traveled Mrs. Hetty Hinds the third. One of the teachers in the dancing school, this strikingly beautiful woman was known there as Miss Maybelle Blossom, but to a few underworld confidants (including Norning no doubt) and to the Chicago police, she was known as "Goldie." So pitifully plain herself, Myrtle felt that her new friend was the most glamorous creature in the whole world, and soon came to adore her. This flood of frank girlish affection greatly pleased the teacher (who also was a very clever actress) and with plans of her own she led Myrtle on, flattering her and pretending to return the girl's affection. What Myrtle didn't know, as she was taken out by the woman, was that she had fallen into the clutches of one of the city's cleverest shoplifters. One day, in a big department store, there was a quick arrest— and Myrtle, an innocent confederate, found herself in prison. She spent six months there, now hating the woman who had caused her downfall. Freed at last, she had wandered out into the country, finally securing steady employment at the pet farm, telling simply that she had been reared in an orphanage but now had to shift for herself. Mrs. Beesaddle probably shrewdly suspected more, but in her kindly way wanted to give the homeless girl another chance, so hired her. Myrtle soon came to love Mrs. Beesaddle dearly. Then came the memorable night of Mrs. Hinds' arrival, with her fake jewelry and rented poodles, all in keeping with Norning's scheme —though I hardly think myself that he expected her to make her telegram sound so important. I've always felt she overdid that. You can easily see now why Myrtle ran away. If she stayed and faced her old enemy, the story of her own imprisonment would come out. She didn't want this known—she rightly felt too that the farm in some way was in danger, and in gratitude to her employers intended to ward off this danger if she possibly could.

And here's what she did: The first night and day after her flight she hid in the barn. There she overheard us talking about the dead poodle and its effect on the farm's business. That gave her the truth. Getting my bicycle the second night, she dug up the dead poodle and took it into town where she had the carcass examined by a veterinarian. Through him she learned that the dog had indeed been poisoned, just as she had suspected. But she couldn't bring herself to come to us with her story of the poisoned poodle, as that would require telling more. So she worked out a daring scheme of her own. Mrs. Hinds found a note in her cabin, telling her vaguely if she wanted to escape arrest to meet the writer of the note at dusk in the old Windmere house in the woods. The note's writer, of course, was Myrtle herself, who set a trap for the woman at the old hotel and held her a prisoner there. It was all done, of course, to get the woman away from the farm and stop her stories and further possible poisoning. In fact, Myrtle did exactly what Norning suspected us of doing. How it all would end, the girl didn't know, and the uncertainty worried her. She and her prisoner were hidden in the old hotel the night we fought the Strickers there. It was Myrtle, of course, who got the marshmallows. Following the arrest of the spy and Norning's flight, Myrtle came back to the farm, tearfully telling all. The five poodles were returned to Chicago, and with their pretended owner in prison, too, for her part in the scheme, and her car confiscated by the police, the case ended. You know all about Norning's scheme; you know why he sent Mrs. Hinds (I'll still call her that) to the farm; you know all that followed there, as the woman cleverly carried out her part; you know about the final arrests. So that ends that. We were misled by a lot of our imaginative ideas, but as you know the truth about everything I won't go into that any more. Even the best detectives are often misled on a case. It is by talking over logical possibilities that a good detective finally gets at the truth.

CHAPTER XX

MYRTLE'S TRIUMPH

AMONG the first of our old renters to come back, with the settling of the harmful stories about the farm, were Mr. and Mrs. Clarabel. They had a trailer this time, having bought a lot more old furniture. Mr. Clarabel, too, had picked up a huge bullfrog somewhere. The first night we heard it we thought someone was in camp with a big bass fiddle. The frog hardly stirred during the daytime, but as soon as dusk fell it got on the floating board in its tub and let loose. "Rum-m-mf! Rum-m-mf! Rum-m-mf!" And every time there was a "Rum-m-mf!" from the tub, Mr. Clarabel would give another "Rum-m-mf!" from his front porch. His wife had seventeen cat-fits over it, the two I guess finally coming to a secret understanding about it, for one day the frog disappeared and after that and all through her stay, Mrs. Clarabel was as sweet as pie to him. Never another cross word! They stayed till the middle of August, Mrs. Clarabel giving each of us five dollars when they left.

"Oh, dear!" she fluttered around. "You can't imagine how I hate to leave here. I've had a wonderful summer here. I haven't been through half the old homes around here either, with their antiques. So you can figure on seeing me back next summer."

"I hate to leave, too," drawled Mr. Clarabel, with a twinkle in his eye. "It's been a big treat to me to eat someone else's cooking. I'll have to do my own cooking again when I get home."

"Fiddlesticks!" snapped his wife. "I still say you can't fry eggs."

"Captain Danglers and I together can," he declared. "We're good cooks when we work together."

At that Mrs. Clarabel gave me a knowing wink. *She* knew the truth!

They drove off then, their dog barking, the trailer swaying, and Mr. Clarabel waving. Gee! It was like losing a member of the family.

Others who came back to their old cabins, in time, were the Cookbook Woman and Red's friend, the Pekingese woman. But he hadn't anything to kick about—all the easy money he earned that summer reading to Whoopee. By the end of the summer he could rattle off the story of Little Red Riding Hood without a single misplaced word.

The good reports that Mrs. Beesaddle got of the farm got her up in a hurry. Brought home finally, she went around for a few weeks in a wheel chair, then going on a cane until finally she was as well as ever. While she was in the chair Horse Foot had the job of pushing her around. Nor was it any slow easy push either, such as invalids usually get. That wasn't her nature at all. "Come! Come!" she kept telling him sharply. "Don't go to sleep back there." He finally got so he could whizz her around at great speed. I always was scared myself that he'd tip her over, but somehow she managed to

keep her balance.   And just as she kept *him* on the
jump, she also kept the rest of us on the jump, Mrs.
Kelly included, who had complete charge of the
kitchen now, Captain Danglers' silly pretense there
having ended in a hurry with the owner's return.
In starting there, Mother had said I could stay a
few weeks, but it turned out that I stayed the whole
summer.   I earned almost a hundred dollars, Peg
earning even more than a hundred, which was swell
for him as he buys all his own clothes.

When Scoop got back, Red and I took up our sta-
tion in the poodle parlor, as there wasn't enough
bellboy work for all of us.   We put out the sign,
JERRY TODD'S POODLE PARLOR, Mrs. Beesaddle turning over all the pet-washing and pet-
brushing jobs in the camp to us.   I could tell a hundred funny stories of our poodle parlor work, if I
had the space.   With this daily fun and the fun we
had nights playing tricks on the Strickers (and getting tricks played on us in return!), I honestly think
that was the happiest summer of my whole life.

Mrs. Topple (as I'll continue to call her) stayed
with us till the last week in June, leaving the day
after the exciting presentation of our radio play.   I
call it "our" play, because we all were in it, Horse
Foot included.

Following that first domino game, Mrs. Topple
often called on me to play with her, so I got to know
her real well.   One evening, when she was talking
about her grandchildren as usual, she let slip that
she was indeed the wealthy Mrs. Harriet Stone,
with a string of breakfast food factories scattered
through the Middle West, just as we had suspected.

She had a little radio in her cabin, and always at a certain hour in the evening she turned the radio on to listen to one of her own breakfast food programs. Her firm had several programs on the air, she told me, but she particularly liked this program because her grandchildren listened to it.

During the program one night she snapped it off disappointedly.

"What trash!" she complained. "I'll have to write to my son to change it. It was a good program when it started—but with those thugs in it now and all that other exciting stuff, it isn't fit for children to hear."

"If you're going to change it," I told her eagerly, "why don't you take our play? Myrtle's swell in it. I bet you'll like it when you hear it. It would make a swell radio serial."

"Humph!" grunted the old lady, with a slight frown. "Did Miss Garton tell you to tell me that?"

"Why, no!" I stared.

"I met Miss Garton in the city and went through several of her plays with her. They were interesting in spots, but in the main too artificial, I thought."

"Well, there's nothing artificial in the play that she has written for us," I declared. "It's really Myrtle's own life story."

"Myrtle is a good girl," came feelingly. "It's unfortunate that she got into that trouble in the city, though I never would hold that against her myself if I had a chance to help her."

"What you ought to do," I daringly carried the suggestion farther, "is to get Miss Garton to write you a whole series of these plays built around

Myrtle and put her in them. The kids will like programs like that, even the boys, for you can have several boys in it, too."

"And you're sure," Mrs. Topple eyed me sharply, "that you haven't talked this over with Miss Garton herself?"

"Absolutely not," I waggled.

"When I first saw Miss Garton here I thought she had followed me down to try to further corner me with her plays. I guess though she just ran across me by accident."

"I can tell you how she found out you were here," I declared.

"How was that, Jerry?"

"She came down to spend the day with her aunt, Mrs. Dartling. I overheard the two talking about their radio plays. Miss Garton said she was going to get some firm like yours to sponsor the plays."

"She didn't know then that I was hiding here under an assumed name, did she?"

"No. But she guessed it when she saw Captain Danglers go by. She found in our guest book, too, that you two came at almost the same time."

"Oh, I see! That's how she found out. A very clever young woman, I should say! Having encountered Danglers in my office and finding him here, she rightly jumped to the conclusion that I was here, too. Well, Jerry, we'll wait and see how your play turns out. Maybe, through it, I can help this little girl here, and Miss Garton, too. Having discovered me here as she did, I can hardly blame the young woman for staying, with the hope of finally interesting me in her work. That is ambition, and I like it. But, Jerry, see that you don't repeat everything you hear here."

I never quite dared asked Mrs. Topple about her trip to the little cemetery. It's my opinion though that she just happened to pass through there in one of her odd night rambles. I did learn though that Captain Danglers was a distant relative of hers, and actually came from the sea. With his bluster, he made a good bodyguard for her. He sure was an odd old man!

It's a little thing, but I suppose I should tell you that with Norning's flight, all trouble over the old hotel lumber stopped.

And now to finish, with an account of our play. At the last moment it was decided to give the play on an outside stage, around which the required seats were built. An electrician from Ashton put in the microphones and amplifiers. Invitations had been sent out to all the surrounding farmers, so we had a large enthusiastic crowd. Mrs. Topple had her son come down to see the play, which went off so well, with Myrtle in the title rôle, that she and Miss Garton were immediately put under contract, one to provide the plays, which will start in Chicago this coming fall, and the other to star in them.

It makes me feel good all over to be able to close my story with this good news about Myrtle. It was her loneliness at the orphanage, and her yearning to have someone to care for her like other little girls that developed in her those imaginative Fairy Caterpillar ideas. In Chicago, she is going on with her dancing and maybe some day she will indeed be known the world over as the Great Myrtleova.

Peg says all she needs is a new face—but I think myself that a little clever make-up will fix that O.K.

When she gets to be world famous, I'll be able to brag that one romantic summer evening I could have had the honor of walking with her in the moonlight, if my feet hadn't hurt me.   Oh-oh!

My new book, coming soon, will be a hilarious outdoor story—JERRY TODD'S CUCKOO CAMP.   With its crazy galloping fun and shivery mystery, I think you'll like it a lot, as we're all in— the whole bunch of us—and you'll find a lot of dandy surprises in it, too.

So, until we meet in the next book—so-long, everybody!

THE END

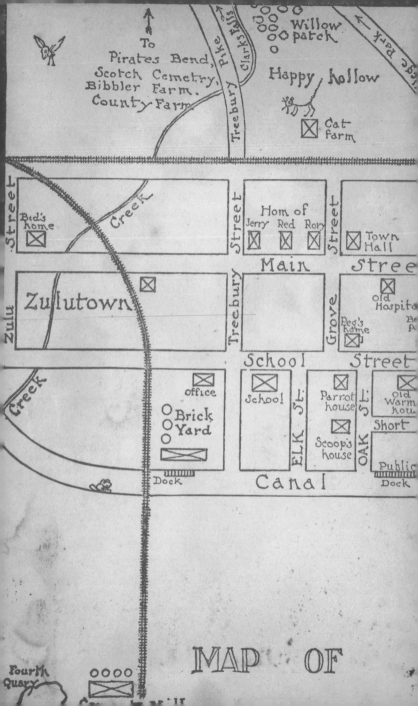